ZACK'S STORY

on life, love and everything

D0334352

ABOUT THE AUTHOR

Abidemi Sanusi was born in Nigeria and now lives in the UK. A keen runner, Abidemi is also the editor of www.christianwriter.co.uk. You can find out more about her on her personal website: www.abidemisanusi.co.uk.

DEDICATION/ACKNOWLEDGEMENTS

This book is dedicated to the people of Liberia and the victims of civil wars everywhere.

All but one character in this book are fictitious. I had the pleasure of meeting Mark Kroeker, Police Commissioner, United Nations Mission in Liberia, on one of my visits to Liberia. His character is real but the words in the book are mine. I've taken creative licence, as all writers do.

My thanks to Lin Ball and everyone at Scripture Union for their hard work on this book. And my thanks to the Holy Spirit: when I am weak, You are strong.

ZACK'S STORY

on life, love and everything

ABIDEMI SANUSI

ZACK'S STORY

Published by Scripture Union,
207–209 Queensway, Bletchley, MK2 2EB, England.

Scripture Union: Scripture Union is an international Christian charity working with churches in more than 130 countries providing resources to bring the good news about Jesus Christ to children, young people and families – and to encourage them to develop spiritually through the Bible and prayer. As well as providing a network of volunteers, staff and associates who run holidays, church-based events and school Christian groups, SU produces a wide range of publications and supports those who use the resources through training programmes.

Email: info@scriptureunion.org.uk

Internet: www.scriptureunion.org.uk

First published 2006

ISBN 1 84427 192 7

Scripture quotations taken from the HOLY BIBLE, TODAY'S NEW INTERNATIONAL VERSION © TNIV © 2001, 2005, by International Bible Society. Used by permission.

British Library Cataloguing-in-Publication Data: a catalogue record for this book is available from the British Library.

Cover design and photography by Phil Grundy

Internal design and typesetting by Creative Pages: www.creativepages.co.uk

Printed and bound in Great Britain by Creative Print and Design (Wales) Ebbw Vale

ZACK'S STORY

on life, love and everything

Intro

It started ten years ago at a riotous university party. A few hours earlier, my then girlfriend told me she'd aborted our child. Without consulting me. I didn't even know she was pregnant. She said it was her third abortion. I didn't know that either. She wouldn't tell me much else after that. Except why she did it. Oh, she told me that, alright. She didn't want 'it'... it was her body... she could do what she liked with it... Then she told me a few things about me. That I was a control freak... I made her feel inadequate. I might be a law scholarship student, she said, but I still had a lot to learn about women and their right to live life the way they chose. And – the final clincher – she was glad she did 'it' because I would've made her keep 'it' and held her against her will.

I didn't hesitate. I walked out of her flat and headed for the student union bar. I wasn't looking for a drink – I was teetotal. But I needed the noise to distract me. I didn't want to go to my flat where I would be alone. The other unlikely alternative that flashed into my mind was to take a chainsaw to her neck and watch her bleed in much the way she'd killed our child.

She. Her. I struggle to say her name. From that day I tended to refer to her as 'that woman'. After all, her name was very inappropriate.

From the student union bar I went on to the party, primarily for one purpose. No strings sex. The only temporary panacea available to numb the physical and emotional pain I felt. I knew there would be lots of women willing to provide such a service at the party.

As it happens, there *were* lots of women. But only one saw my bleeding heart and she wouldn't sleep with me.

So that's how I met Kemi. The minute I walked into the room, I was drawn to her. Kemi was vivacious and spontaneous. So unlike me. I didn't say much. Just listened. She was an only child and very close to her family, immediate and extended. That much was quickly established by her many references to her parents and her 'crazy cousin Foluke' that night.

Ten years later, she's still talking and I'm still listening. She's my shining star.

Kemi was glowing, bright-eyed, bubbly, loud. With curly, unruly hair that she tugged at without mercy. She told me it was the bane of her life, that all mixed-race children are cursed with this blessing. She had the natural confidence of someone who knew who they were and where they were going. Within minutes I wanted to go there with her, wherever that place was.

So I didn't get any sex that night, but I found Kemi. We were 'just friends' for a couple of years after that, and then we started dating. And then... she became a Christian. She banned me from her bed and her heart because I was an unbeliever. I was devastated. But a year later, still a Christian, somehow she came to me of her own volition. And then decided to abort the child she frighteningly found she was carrying – *our* child – because, well, it just wasn't convenient.

I definitely wasn't going to let that happen to me again! I threatened her with a lawsuit. After a lot of heartache, we were reconciled, had our baby and I asked her to marry me.

So, as I write these words, Kemi and I have been married for two years, although we have known each other for ten. Today, she is an advertising honcho. One of the best in her field. Her *Singing Diapers* advertising campaign is generally considered to be one of the biggest and most successful in UK history. While I, a corporate lawyer assigned to my firm's most lucrative brief, ended up at the centre of an international scandal and became a full-time house husband. Sure, I help people out in church with 'legal stuff'. Sometimes I write.

Sometimes I'm delusional. I dream of being another John Grisham. After all, we're both ex-lawyers. And we both have an expressed faith. He is a firm and card-carrying member of the Baptist tradition. It took me a long hard two years but today I am a fully fledged member of the Pentecostal tradition – noise and all. My other similarity with Mr Grisham is my desire to put pen to paper. I have a need to share my story.

Writing this is not just for the entertainment of unknown readers, but for my son: Yanis Woboluwamitito Kariba, otherwise know as Yanis T. In laying everything out on paper, I am giving him the truth about himself, his father and the events of his early life. Is there another reason? Perhaps, in telling my story, I lay my past to rest and look to the future with freedom and relief.

Perhaps you're wondering about my son's name. The Nigerian part of the name, Woboluwamitito, means, 'See how big my God is.' Yanis is a Hebrew name which means 'Gift of God'. Some more genealogy: my wife Kemi is half Nigerian and half British white. Her father Femi is from the Yoruba tribe and her mother Gail is from London. As for me, let's just say that for most of my life I believed that I was half black and half mid-eastern. Truth is, I didn't know anything much about myself; not my race, my date of birth, nothing. I was left outside a children's home when I was barely 48 hours old and was given the last name of the woman who found me. But, I'm getting ahead of myself.

Let me begin my story.

Yanis T popped out of his mother's womb like a scrawny multicoloured chicken. I can still remember the statistics: weight 3.2 kilos or pretty much seven pounds, length 19 inches, head circumference 13 inches, Apgar test score a perfect 10, parents' fatigue level sky-high.

Yanis T caused quite a stir in the hospital. I'd been told that all babies look pale, more pink and Caucasian, when they're born. Not my son. His skin colour and hair were – for lack of a better word – indeterminate. He looked Mediterranean, with strange but beautiful frizzy hair. His mother called him a 'rainbow coalition'.

'Like an American. Did you know it's quite possible for an American to have a mix of no less than six races in them?'

'Well, in England, the word for people like him is *other*,' I replied.

Already, I was getting anxious. I didn't want my son suffering the same kind of worries I did when I filled out ethnic monitoring forms. Not knowing my parents made me an indeterminate race and I wasn't keen on having racial blood tests. Who knows what those could throw up?

'His mother *also* caused a stir when she was born,' my father-in-law Femi announced proudly at the bedside.

'Only because you were strutting up and down like a peacock announcing to everyone who would care to listen that your daughter would be the first black prime minister of Britain,' Kemi retorted.

'Well, she's not so far off now, being as she's heading the biggest and most successful advertising campaign in the UK!'

My father-in-law grinned at me. 'Well, son... Everything changes from this moment. You're now a father and nothing is more important than that little bundle of joy you have in your hands.'

Femi didn't voice it, but I knew the underlying agenda to his affirming words. He was pleading with me to understand why he had supported Kemi's initial decision to abort my son, his grandchild. This same grandchild that he was cooing over could have been a bundle of mangled limbs had it not been for the desperate action I took to preserve his life. I felt a momentary flash of anger towards him, but recalled Pastor Michael's words to me not too long ago. *Let it go, Zack, let it go.*

I drew in a deep breath and turned my attention to Kemi.

'We'll be okay,' I promised.

'Of course, you'll both be okay. You have a beautiful boy,' Gail, my mother-in-law said.

'*Was* heading the most successful campaign in the UK,' Kemi said.

'Pardon?' Femi asked.

'I said I *was* heading the most successful advertising campaign in the UK. *Was*, dad,' Kemi repeated, not looking at me.

By early March, a month after his birth, Yanis T had filled out all over. With his podgy thighs and arms, he looked like a thoroughly edible and exotic German sausage. And I could not get enough of him. Everything he did fascinated me. Even when he released one of the most potent bodily emissions known to man! In fact, I became overly obsessed with his bodily fluids for a while, one minute anxious that his insides were a hardening mass, the next convinced he was suffering from a tropical disease.

I was prone to other strange behaviour as well. Like putting my finger under his nose to feel his breath, to reassure myself that he was indeed still breathing. Many were the nights I would sit by his bed and watch him, terrified he would be a victim of cot death or something else harmful that I would be powerless to prevent. I think that was what scared me the most. Being powerless. And that was part of a bigger fear. It seemed I'd spent my whole life fighting powerlessness. My childhood circumstances were programmed to ensure that people like me failed.

I found it ironic that someone as small as my son was a reminder of how thoroughly helpless his big strong dad was to control anything in his life. Though I could stay up all night watching him if I wanted to, the truth was that I could not guard him 24/7. This knowledge did not fully dawn on me until much later, when Yanis T was about 18 months old and he inserted his wet fingers into a live socket. But, back before the Socket Incident, I really did think I could be his 24-hour guardian angel. After the Socket Incident, I reconciled myself to my human limitations. I wanted to protect my son from harm but the truth was that I couldn't do it. Not without turning myself and Kemi into nervous wrecks. And certainly not without making God redundant. I still watch over him though. Just in case.

But I'm getting ahead of myself again. Through our son's early weeks, Kemi and I continued to feel exhausted. My son *consumed* time. Leaving the house required military-style planning that incorporated all the 'what ifs' that Gail insisted probably wouldn't be, involving supplies of nappies, powder, cream, feeding bottles for expressed milk and at least one change of clothes for Yanis.

One day I suggested a family outing to the park down the road.

'Just a 10-minute walk,' I said.

Kemi refused. She would much rather have a nap and some time to herself, she said. I told her she needed fresh air more than she needed the nap. Eventually she agreed. It took us thirty minutes to leave the house, by which time Yanis T had become rather fractious.

Three hours later, a screaming baby and two extremely distressed parents ended up at the paediatric wing of the local hospital, emerging one hour afterwards feeling rather foolish amid the knowing smiles of the hospital staff. Yanis had colic. Many babies have it. It clears up by itself, usually in the third month. No one knows the cause and, no, there is no known cure.

'You just have to ride it out,' the paediatrician said.

When we got home, Kemi swore never to leave the house again until Yanis was, at the very least, five years old.

Gail and Femi said we would miss these early days once they'd gone. I knew they were right. In the meantime, I had more pressing issues to ponder on. One of them, without being coy about it, was sex.

Knowing the religious implications of the sexual act for my fiancée did not make me want it any less. Kemi, being a Pentecostal Christian, didn't believe in sex before marriage and certainly not with an 'unbeliever'. (That's me.)

Patently, she had slept with me in the past. Our pre-marital road to Yanis has been punctuated with lots of Christian guilt (from Kemi) and gut-wrenching pain (from me) as she veered between her faith and her love for me. At one point she made up her mind that she would have me *and* Jesus. She didn't want to choose between the two of us and she didn't see why she had to.

Those were painful times for both of us. I didn't understand why her faith seemed to cause her so much unhappiness and struggle. Her vociferous proclamations that life without Jesus was pointless seemed, even to me, to clash incongruously with many of her actions. Inevitably, she resented the guilt induced by her faith. And finally decided, once again, to ban me from her bed.

To cut a long story short, I asked Kemi to marry me a week before Yanis T was born and she said yes. I knew it was partly because she believed I was close to making my own 'commitment to Jesus'. For the record, I wasn't. Really. But I had agreed to regular meetings with Pastor Michael and

Mark, new husband to the lovely blonde Vanessa, Kemi's long-time best friend.

But, anyway, to return to the absence of sexual relations. It had been months. And somehow Pastor Michael's earnest conversations about channelling my energies towards more 'productive' activities seemed lame. He'd been married for ever so I think he had forgotten what life is like in the real world. All the 'productive' activities in the world did not change the fact that I wanted to sleep with my fiancée and the mother of my baby and I couldn't because she didn't believe (despite evidence to the contrary) in sex before marriage. Somehow the abstinence didn't seem to bother her. Her time was consumed with our son and sometimes I wondered if she would ever want me again.

One morning, as I made faces at my son over the side of the cot, he squinted at me and smiled. It wasn't wind; I was sure it was a real smile! I made more faces and he gave me more smiles. Then I leaned over his sleepy mother.

'I'm off,' I said, kissing her cheek.

'Do you have to go?'

'Someone has to bring home the bacon,' I replied.

Kemi got off the bed very grudgingly.

'I feel like I'm going to be doing this and feeling like this all my life... not having the energy to have a shower, having your son permanently latched on to these pendulous things... and feeling very, very fat.'

'You're the lovely mother of my wonderful child. And you're not fat. You're wholesome.'

'Wholesomely fat. I am a wholesomely fat hausfrau.'

I kissed her again and left the flat. I sent her a text as I reached the tube station. *I love wholesome hausfraus.* She texted me back. *Liar.*

I got to my office at 8.30am. Maxine, the colleague at the desk opposite mine, flashed me a smile.

'How's the baby?'

'Yanis. His name is Yanis and he's fine.'

'Yanis. Let's see the picture again.' She slid over to my desk and peered over the latest photo of Yanis stuck onto the side of my computer. I couldn't help but notice several things: 1) that the first two buttons of her shirt were undone; 2) that she somehow managed to lean towards me and Yanis' photo at the same time; and 3) that our colleague Andy had a stupid grin on his face. When she finished looking, she stood up gracefully, smoothed imaginary ruffles on her skirt and sashayed back to her desk.

She knew what she was doing, alright. I declared war on my traitorous thoughts and commanded my senses to face the present situation.

'Kemi is fine as well,' I said.

'Of course.'

Andy got up and made his way to the washroom, his hands covering his mouth and his shoulders shaking. I called Kemi. I could hear my son bawling in the background. *How could someone so small let out such almighty cries?* It did not seem biologically possible. I told Kemi I would try to be home on time and said goodbye. A feature on Liberia on the day's *Financial Times* lying on my desk had caught my eye. *Africa's first and forgotten republic*, the heading said. I started reading.

Despite its vast mineral resources, Liberia remains one of the poorest countries in the world. Fourteen years of civil war stoked by mercenaries, its own government and outside factors have conspired to make this country financially and developmentally moribund. Today, Liberia's literacy rate remains at 10 per cent, with some arguing that the figure is a lot lower. A generation of children have grown up knowing only war. There are no electricity, water or telephone lines in the country and there haven't been for the last 15 years.

Although the 2003 civil war has officially been declared over, much remains to be done in the country. Of particular significance to foreign interests are Liberia's timber, diamonds, iron ore and shipping certificates. The UN had imposed a ban on trade in Liberia's diamonds as they were used in exchange for arms by the then President Charles Taylor in his wars in the sub-region. There is speculation that some private interests are in the process of bidding for Liberia's diamond mining sector. Attempts to confirm this with the Liberian transitional government spokesperson have so far proved futile.

I made a mental note to contact the reporter. Something was brewing in Liberia. And it was only a matter of time before my bank – Rhodenburg – would get involved as an investment bank with a specialisation in emerging economies. High risk but infinitely higher returns. I was expecting a summons to the director's office all day but it didn't come.

Just before the end of the working day, I googled a name: The Florence Nightingale Children's Home. Scanning the results quickly, I sent off an impulsive email. Then I went home.

* * *

The least of you will become a thousand, the smallest a mighty nation. I am the LORD; in its time I will do this swiftly (Isaiah 60:22).

I shook my head and closed the book. Kemi smiled at me. My son was, as always, at her breast. His eyes were closed. I envied him his unrestricted access to his mother.

'Zack, don't.'

'Don't what?'

'I saw you... look at me.'

'I look at you all the time.' I sighed.

'Tell me what you just read.'

'Something about a mighty nation and the Lord acting swiftly. These prophets or whoever... they don't make it easy to understand, do they? And you wonder why I'm not interested in church? If you were confronted with something like that, would you run to church?'

Kemi knew I was joking, but my words were not entirely without truth. My periodic dips into the Bible threw up statements such as the one I'd just read with increasing frequency. Despite what Kemi said about the relevance of the Bible to real life, those statements seemed to me to prove my point about the Bible's complete *irrelevance*.

But I had made up my mind to do one small thing. I crossed the living room and sat next to her on the sofa.

'I think it's time I became a Christian.'

'Really? I mean, thank God!' Kemi said. Though her voice was enthusiastic, her face was sceptical.

'Wasn't this what you wanted,' I asked, watching her face.

'It is. It just took me by surprise, that's all.'

She motioned for me to come closer and I did. Yanis made sucking noises. We both laughed and Kemi kissed my cheek.

'Thank you,' she said. 'Nothing will ever be the same again – the way you think, the way you do things. Being a Christian's a whole new different world, Zack.'

'If I didn't know better, I would think you were trying to put me off.'

'Of course not. I just want you to be clear about what you're letting yourself in for. You understand about the sinner's prayer?'

'Yes. Mark and Michael explained it to me. It's when you ask Jesus to be your Saviour.'

Kemi nodded in approval.

'You understand about sin, Jesus' death, his resurrection... '

I rolled my eyes. This wasn't the time for a theology session.

'Can we just get on with it?'

'We still can't... can't have sex before marriage.'

'I know, I know! Even if I don't understand what the big deal is about pre-marital sex. One thing at a time. My sinner's prayer will speed up our journey to the altar and eventually to our matrimonial bed. Right?'

Kemi put her arms around my neck and kissed me on the lips.

'You truly are a miracle, Zachary Kariba.'

And so it was that on March 16th I held my fiancée's hands and recited the sinner's prayer after her.

I waited and waited. I didn't know what I was expecting: angels, thunder and lightning, or at least a blinding light with a drumroll. I got none of those things, but I did get something that made me glad I said the prayer: Kemi's face. She was so happy that I was finally 'saved'.

3

'Happy wedding day! How do you feel?'

'Like Zachary Kariba.'

'Aw, look at you two. You make a lovely couple!'

'It's only taken eight years... '

It was a Saturday in April, a warm spring day. We drove from the registry office to my in-laws' house for a reception where I was surrounded by Kemi's relatives – more than 50 of them. I counted the number of people that represented me, the groom. Four. Exactly how an 'other' with no familial ties would be represented at a wedding.

But not for long, I thought silently to myself, remembering the exchange of emails with the children's home. I had taken the first step towards finding out who I was, starting with a search for my mother. She held all the answers, I was sure. I had to find her.

I hadn't told Kemi about this. She would probably talk me out of it, thinking she was protecting me from disappointment. Also, Yanis kept her fully occupied. She was still trying to find her feet around the motherhood maze and I didn't want to add to her worry list.

The truth was, I couldn't live with the secrets any longer. I had to know. I was a father now. I wanted Yanis to know his paternal roots. What if my parents had genetic traits that could have medical repercussions for my baby son? As his father, it was my job to protect him and make him aware of any threats to his life, real or perceived. And, as much as I hated to admit it to myself, I envied my wife. I was jealous of her close attachment to her family, especially Femi's colourful relatives. Wherever they were, they made sure people knew who they were: the Smith family. I knew they had genuine love and affection for me but it just wasn't the same as having my own relatives.

I did not let myself think of one possible outcome: that my mother might not want to be found. That couldn't be. She probably left me outside the children's home to protect me. Perhaps she had been a teenage mother. Or maybe, like my wife's parents, she fell in love with someone outside her race and took drastic action to protect herself and me. Whatever the circumstances of my birth, once I found her, I planned I would tell her I harboured no ill towards her; I just wanted to meet her; to know who she was and, in the process, learn who I was. I would also ask her about my father – who he was, how they met.

I stopped myself. As usual, I was getting carried away. Reconciliation plans were a little premature.

I looked at my wife at the reception. She looked wholesomely beautiful. I kissed her with the relief of a man who knew his days in the sexual wilderness were over.

'Zack, behave yourself!'

It was Vanessa, my wife's best friend. She herself had been married just four months earlier.

'Yes, the church wedding – the blessing – is still to come,' Mark, Vanessa's husband added.

'Yes. But today we are legally married. With all the benefits attached to it!' I winked at him.

He laughed. Gail fussed over Kemi while her father kissed the top of her head. I took my son from Vanessa and held him close to me. *Wherever and whoever you are, God, thanks for this – my son and wife.*

'Smile.' The photographer held his camera high above his head.

We all smiled. The camera clicked.

* * *

Richard Littleton, company director and my line manager, gave the document in front of him a tap.

'I assume that you've all read this report. Just to recap... Liberia's just ended a civil war and things are not looking very pretty over there. The country, its economy, in fact *everything* is in ruins, as would be the case in any post-war country. But Liberia has something to its credit; something that has been one of the causes of war in the country for the last 14 years. Diamonds!

'It also has other resources, like its internationally renowned quality timber. And Liberia is host to the largest latex plantation in the world. But we are not interested in wood or rubber.

'Our sources tell us that we are in the running for an open tender for Liberia's diamond mines. They call it an open tender but in reality they're only considering bids from five banks, Rhodenburg included. This will not be like other bids. With this bid, we will be *bidding with a heart*, primarily because of the state of affairs in Liberia. There is a transitional government in place. Whatever we offer has to be so good the democratic government elected next year will have no choice but to offer Rhodenburg sole rights to all its diamond mines. We'll be doing some charity stuff – building schools, training teachers... the kind of stuff that makes us look like Oxfam. You know the drill.'

Richard fixed each one of us in turn with an unblinking stare.

'Don't underestimate the publicity this is going to stir up. I've got word that there are a few do-gooders who are against this bid on moral grounds. They argue that so-called blood diamonds or conflict diamonds have been the cause of war in some countries in Africa for the last 30 years, hence nobody should be bidding for sole rights to any country's diamonds.

'The fact is, nobody wants to take on Liberia. Not the World Bank, not the IMF and certainly not the Americans. It's in chronic international debt. The only people interested in Liberia are mercenary companies that offer to secure the diamond mines and head off external threats in return for exclusive mining rights, much as has been done in Sierra Leone, Angola and the Congo.

'The difference between us and these mercenary companies

is our *transparency*. We are an investment company – and nothing more. We do not trade diamonds for arms or any of the other stuff that has plagued Liberia since diamonds were discovered there.'

There were nods from Maxine, Andy and some of the others around the room. Richard continued.

'We have a chance to make history in Liberia. Zack, I want you to be the lead legal counsel on this. Andy will be your strategist and Maxine your finance expert. In three weeks, all three of you will be in Liberia. James: you'll provide backup from here. Official reason for trip: feasibility study. Unofficial: sniffing out the competition and potential partners. You will be going via Nigeria as there are no direct flights to Liberia. Any questions?'

He looked around. The room was quiet.

'Good. Meeting over. Zack, I want to see you in my office.'

I followed him and he indicated for me to take the seat across from his wide desk.

'I'm sure I don't need to tell you how important this is. If we pull this off, you will be in line for promotion as 'Legal Director – Emerging Economies (Africa)'.

'I know.'

He mentioned our bidding competitors.

'We can't afford to lose out to them. This is not just a bid about Liberia and revitalising its economy. That may be the official line, but it's not our line. This is about that whole sub-region. The finance sector is as yet an undiscovered gold mine. We need to get in there, risks and all, just like we did with the former Russian states. Just like we did with China and the tiger economies. We got into those places *first*. That's why their governments and those in the know prefer to work with us. Because we went in there and took risks for them when no one else would. If there is a bid for Liberia's mining sector under the guise of revitalising its economy, then bid we must with the best of them. The difference is that we are bidding for West Africa's finance sector.

'Our aim is to be the biggest investment bank in West Africa and ultimately Africa. They said it couldn't be done in China and the tiger economies but we proved them wrong. And we will prove them wrong again in Liberia and West Africa. That's the bigger picture I want you to be looking at.'

I listened intently. Richard was in his forties, married to his childhood sweetheart and with three children. He didn't drink, smoke or indulge in any of the excesses that characterised the lives of so many who worked in the City. I liked him. He was one of the four people representing the bridegroom at my wedding.

'And, by the way, you're going to be famous, Zack. You'll be profiled in tomorrow's FT. The countdown to the bid starts now and you're the face of this bank. Don't let me down.' His mobile rang and I left his office.

I went straight to the washroom and stood in front of the big mirror. I did that sometimes. Perhaps to remind myself that the person staring back at me was indeed Zachary Kariba, legal hotshot, en route to making history at the bank as its youngest ever legal director. I'd come a long way. A nobody of indeterminate race with no familial history playing with the big guys. Still looking at the mirror, I straightened my tie, smoothed my jacket and stood that little bit taller.

Zachary Kariba, who are you?

I am a corporate lawyer.

Zachary Kariba, who are you?

I am married to a beautiful woman with a beautiful baby boy.

Zachary Kariba, who are you?

I don't know. I am a man floundering in the dark, looking for answers.

I went back to my desk. Maxine looked up as I passed.

'Let me guess. He talked about promotion.'

I didn't answer. There was an email from the Florence Nightingale Children's Home in my inbox.

* * *

Yanis was lying on a blanket on the floor and Kemi was sitting on the sofa staring down at him. The flat was in chaos.

'I'm sorry. I didn't have time to clean up,' Kemi said when she saw my grimace. I couldn't help it.

23

'You could've tried,' I said.

'Mum and Vanessa were meant to come round and give me a hand... '

'You're a married woman now,' I snapped. 'Surely it's time you stopped running to your parents every time you graze your knee.'

My wife didn't say a word. She laid Yanis on the sofa and started tidying the living room. When she finished, she stood in front of me and threw a bundle of Yanis' soiled clothes at me.

'He's your son too, so you might do some picking up after him.'

She stormed off, slamming the bedroom door behind her. Yanis whimpered. I picked him up and put him on my shoulder, holding him with one hand while I loosened my tie. He burped and drooled on my shirt. I kissed him and patted his back. My heart filled up with love for him as I inhaled his milky baby scent. The day's stress started melting away. Even the email lost its fearful hold over me.

Kemi appeared in the doorway. She had her coat on.

'Kemi, I'm sorry. I had a... a trying day at work. Richard—'

The front door slammed. She was gone. Two hours later she burst back in, hardly taking time to get inside the flat before letting out a stream of words.

'My office called today. Windy CEO is getting anxious about World Star Baby. They said he reminded them all that *I* was the reason we landed the Singing Diapers campaign in the first place.'

Windy CEO was Kemi's rude but affectionate name for the Singing Diapers UK chief with a flatulence problem who was one of her biggest fans.

She gave me no time to reply but charged into the bedroom. Yanis let out a squeal.

'I think he's ready for a feed,' I called after her. My wholesome wife gave me a rather unwholesome reply.

4

So there is hope for your future, declares the LORD. Your children will return to their own land (Jeremiah 31:17).

Reading the day's devotional Bible verse later that evening as I got ready for bed made my thoughts turn immediately to the latest email from the children's home. The verse also took me back to the hellish weeks when Kemi was pregnant with Yanis T but wanted to abort him. Having run out of options, that's when I started reading her daily Bible verses, to make sense of her, of it all.

I didn't understand all that I read. But I often felt reassured – don't ask me how – that all would turn out well. And so far, in many ways, it had. Kemi did not go through with the abortion and now we were married. We'd been through a lot in our eight-year history.

Yet right now I knew I wasn't behaving towards her like the wonderful born-again Christian she thought she was married to. I had brought the stress of the day job home and took it out on her. It wasn't right. Nor fair.

I turned to her.

'I'm sorry.'

'It's okay,' she said. 'But I'm trying very hard here, Zack. I need you to cut me some slack.'

'I just wish you weren't such a martyr about it all, about motherhood and everything.'

It wasn't the right thing to say but it had to be said. My wife was behaving like she was the only woman in the world who'd ever had a baby and been stuck at home cleaning up.

Kemi's back stiffened. She turned away from me, lying on the bed facing the wall. Yanis snuffled in his cot.

'I didn't mean that. At least, not in the way you think... '

'You meant it, Zack. You did!'

'I wanted to say... Richard—'

'Good night, Zack.'

She turned off the lamp on her side of the bed. I sighed, feeling defeated and frustrated, and thought about the email again, about Richard, about Liberia and about the Bible verse. It had all seemed so simple. I had it all worked out. Kemi and I would get married and everything would be fine. I would go to work and come home to my wife and son. In winter, we would sit by the fireplace; in summer we would go walking in the park. I was even beginning to think that maybe we would fulfil Kemi's fantasy of being a Christian couple. You know, the kind of couple that go to church every Sunday, pray, spend long hours talking about God and generally doing Jesus stuff. Sure, we would have problems. But nothing was insurmountable. Kemi and I went back a long way. Even better, we loved each other.

There was no doubt in my mind that Kemi and I were meant for each other. She was my bright shining star and I was her rock – calm, reliable and dependable. We were a team, my wife and I. We also had Jesus. Jesus? He was only a vague shadowy figure in my life. But somehow he was starting to come to life, to jump out of the Bible verses I now read every day without fail. True, I didn't understand the stuff about Jesus dying for man's salvation. It seemed unfair to burden mankind with a guilt complex about this issue when we didn't ask for it. Mark and Michael's ramblings about sin resulting in spiritual and eternal separation from God remained just that – ramblings. And as for hell, well, I just could not reconcile somebody supposedly dying for mankind and then sending them to hell just because they don't believe in his self-appointed sacrifice.

I kept my thoughts to myself. Kemi got really freaked out if I started talking like that. She said it was blasphemy. Vanessa reckoned it was my 'pride that's talking'. I had lots of questions. Like, if Jesus was so great and so powerful, why was the world in such a mess?

Because we live in a fallen world and you cannot blame God for man's mess, Kemi would tell me, over and over again. Sometimes through gritted teeth. But it didn't make sense to me.

To annoy her even further, I would ask her who created God.

'Zack, God just *is*,' she would answer impatiently. 'Now pass me the nappy.'

If I really wanted to aggravate her and amuse myself, I would ask her why she did some stuff that was clearly not Christlike. Like let loose her fiery temper. I won't repeat what she said to that.

It wasn't all bad, though. This faith stuff was important to Kemi and, to be fair, some bits of it I did understand and agree with, while other bits of it were just way out there. It seemed to me that Christianity – at least, the Pentecostal and evangelical variety practised by my wife and her church – placed far too many unrealistic burdens on its followers. Mark and Michael's entreaties about God living inside each born-again Christian and empowering them from within just sounded to me just like any other lifestyle movement. Didn't Buddhists and Hindus claim the same thing? Yes, they replied. But true Christianity as laid out in the Bible is *the* only truth. And Christianity is more relationship than religion.

As a lawyer, all that stuff really bothered me because it had fanatical overtones. I prided myself on my rational, moderate behaviour. Vanessa reckoned that if I just put my brain on lockdown I would see the Bible for what it really was.

For Kemi, Mark, Vanessa and their friends, it all made sense. I was still working my way through it and driving everybody crazy in the process with my questions and endless debate. Mark insisted that he didn't mind. He said it prevented him from getting comfortable.

I couldn't sleep. As usual, my mind was running through a very long 'to do' list. Near the top was the December church wedding – the blessing – which was supposed to be a matter of real spiritual significance, but I was struggling with that too. 'Churchspeak' was filled with references to the physical and

27

spiritual world which sounded like goobledy-gook to me. I'd been told our registry office wedding was primarily a practical measure as it wasn't right for two churchgoers to be living together 'in sin' with a child and all. As far as I was concerned I was 'in love' with Kemi, not 'in sin' with her. And I couldn't understand the difference the trip to the registry office made to God.

Then there was the matter of the flat. My bachelor pad. It was really too small for two adults and a baby. It was time we started looking for somewhere bigger. And soon.

And, of course, there was the email from the children's home. I had an appointment with the current director the following week. He said they operated an open policy about records, wherever possible. He could only answer the questions about my past and my time in the home that he was legally obliged to. Nothing more, nothing less. I cursed the law and every legal drama on television that made everyone a lawyer.

Then there was the impending Liberia bid. I'd worked on bids long enough to relish and dread them in equal measure: long hours at the office, regular and gruelling trips to the country and the sheer skullduggery of working in an investment bank that prided itself on operating in countries where no other banks would go.

Today's devotional verse about hope for the future started to taunt me again. Pastor Michael told me to read those verses like they were meant especially for me. *Don't worry if it doesn't make sense. One day, when you least expect it and need it most, those verses will be like water in your spiritual desert.* Like now? The bit about children returning to their homeland. Was that directed at me? I wished it was but concluded not. If all one had to do to make decisions was pick Bible verses at random, then everyone would be doing it. Kemi read the Bible too, but that hadn't stopped her from heading down to the abortion clinic when she first found out she was pregnant with Yanis.

Which brought me to something else. I didn't like it when Kemi and I argued. I reached across the bed and pulled her close to me.

'I'm sorry,' I whispered into her ear and kissed the back of her neck. She was the only thing I had that I could call my own and she'd given me Yanis. They made me complete. She was my shining star and I loved her deeply. Maybe too much. I kissed her neck again. She smelled of baby bath and talcum powder.

'No, you're not. You just don't like it when we argue.'

She paused. Then, 'You didn't even ask about my job.'

I was silent. She knew why I didn't *dare* ask about her job. I was afraid of what she would tell me. I liked having her home with Yanis. I knew she struggled with the idea of staying home with him and putting her career on hold but I couldn't bring myself to talk about it with her. I didn't want to hear what she would tell me.

'Zack, I *have* to go back to work. I worked hard for that campaign. I've just been promoted and you're asking me to give up everything I've worked for to stay home and look after your son.'

'He's also your son.'

This time she was silent. I pulled the bedcover up around my head and slept.

5

The calls came in thick and fast – and so did the ribbing from my colleagues. *GQ* magazine would like to do a feature called *Ethnicity in the City*. I would be the lead story. Was it true I grew up in a children's home? *Marie Claire* wanted an interview with Kemi and me. Some organisation called *Save West Africa* left a message 'of particular importance' on my voicemail. They worked in Liberia with 'disenfranchised people' and wanted to know my bank's policy on corporate social responsibility (CSR). We didn't have one. I made a mental note to get Andy to give the organisation a call.

Our operations in Asia had not generated so much interest in the UK. Perhaps because it seemed farther away. Africa was a continent that tended to provoke rather extreme reactions from people: anger as well as compassion. And now, thanks to Comic Relief and Mr Bob Geldof, everybody had become an expert on Africa. Even the man on the street. This was making it difficult for companies trading in Africa to operate as before – with impunity – as they now faced intense international scrutiny.

This bid would not be like the rest. Our previous bids and work in Asia and former Soviet states were structured to work with the existing financial infrastructure, however weak. Liberia did not have any financial structures. In fact, it did not have any structures at all. Fourteen years of war had made certain of that. In the event we won the bid, we would have to start building everything from scratch: putting in frameworks to rebuild the diamond mining sector, educating and training

Liberians... The high illiteracy rate filled me with particular unease. The list and legal implications were endless.

I was beginning to feel a bit nervous. What did I think I was doing, getting involved with this bid? Did I have any choice? Yet, despite the difficulties, something in me wanted it. What was I trying to prove? Liberia was no place for people like me, now I had a family to think about. What would happen to them if something happened to me while I was out there? My father-in-law did not make me feel any better.

'Forget it,' he said. 'The country's too volatile. The war might be over but that does not mean it's safe. Bid for your directorship somewhere else. Try Chad.'

I told him there weren't any bids for Chad. Liberia was Rhodenburg's way into West Africa. I tried finding something positive on Liberia – to no avail. As countries go, I discovered, it was rather small. The population count was about 3.5 million. Said one hardened war correspondent in the *Guardian* newspaper, *I've reported in 30 out of 54 countries in Africa. From child soldiers in the Congo to girl prostitutes in Sierra Leone, I thought I'd pretty much seen it all and done it all until I went to Liberia. Then I understood the curse of poverty.* Another journalist wrote, *Liberia remains selectively forgotten by the outside world because acknowledging its existence would mean acknowledging our contribution to its current state. The country has been economically and socially raped by its own people and outsiders since the freed slaves landed in the early 1800s.*

I hated to admit it, but it was looking at a really tough assignment. Briefly, I considered pulling out of the project. But I hardened my resolve. I had worked too hard and come too far to let doomsayers affect my bid for professional glory. Rhodenburg was going to win the Liberia bid and I was going to make history at the firm as its youngest ever legal director. End of story.

My mobile rang, jolting me out of my reverie. It was my wife.

'You could've told me about the FT profile. Dad's just called me.'

'I know and I'm sorry. I did try to tell you last night—'

'I'm proud of you.'

'I'm sorry about last night.'

'We'll talk some more when you get home. I love you.'

'I love you too.'

I hung up just as Richard called me, Maxine and Andy into his office. He was looking very pleased.

'Well done, Zack. Nice picture too. What did you think about the children's home bit? I know I didn't ask you but I figured it was a nice touch. Good PR. You're identifying with Liberia's poor because you've been there yourself, blah, blah blah. Hope you didn't mind.'

I did. It was my private life, not his.

He continued. 'I've set up a meeting for the three of you with Janet Williams, a consultant development economist. She's worked all over Africa, in particular Sierra Leone and Angola, so she knows what she's doing.

'And tomorrow you'll all be at *Save West Africa* at 11.30am. You have a meeting with the new director. This meeting is for PR purposes. It looks good to the public to be seen to have do-gooders on our side with this bid. And while you're at it, pick the director's brains. She might have some insider knowledge on Liberia that will come in useful for us. We'll reconvene here at 2.30 tomorrow.

'And another thing. Rhodenburg takes its employees' safety very seriously and don't think for a minute that we're sending you off to Liberia without security backup. Tomorrow afternoon's meeting will address those concerns and give you the opportunity to meet Ben and Martin, the security personnel responsible for your safety while you're there. They've both worked all over the sub-region so they know what they're doing. Any questions? Good. Let's get to it! We have a lot of work to do.'

We shuffled out of Richard's room. Maxine hung back while I picked up some papers.

'Gosh! This is turning out to be quite a ride, isn't it,' she said, smiling in that particular way that women have when they are about to launch an assault on a man's physical senses.

I looked straight ahead, refusing to acknowledge to myself that her too-short skirt displayed her long legs to perfection. I thought of my wholesome wife and son. And finally, I thought of the Bible verse for the day: *Many a man claims to have unfailing love, but a faithful man who can find?* (Proverbs 20:6). I had congratulated myself on reading it that morning because I knew that *I* was a faithful man. Kemi and I had our moments but we both knew I wasn't the type to wander from the hearth. And it wasn't just the fear of the physical damage Kemi would wreak on me if I ever did such a thing! Deep inside, I'm just a boring lawyer with exotic looks who happens to crave familial stability above all else. Having found it with Kemi and now Yanis, I wouldn't trade it for anything. That's why Kemi called me her boring, dependable rock. Maxine could assault my senses all she wanted, but my heart was firmly at home with my wife and child. I focused my mind on the day's Bible verse though. Just to remind my physical senses that I was still boss.

'Yes, quite a ride,' I replied, walking away. I felt I was a marked man but I was determined not to be one of Maxine's victims. She scared me. She didn't join in the gossip about her sexual exploits but the little I heard left me in no doubt as to her plans for me. To think that there had been a time I genuinely believed that we were friends! Kemi was sharper than I was. She cottoned onto Maxine the first moment she met her. In fact, Maxine's gift to Yanis had pride of place at the *bottom* of his wardrobe, right underneath where our shoes were kept. I knew better than to ask my wife if Yanis would ever wear the cute little dungarees.

'Well done on the profile,' Maxine called out after me.

I didn't answer. I kept on walking. When I got to my desk, Andy sidled over.

'Most men in this office would give anything to be in your shoes. The hottest girl in this company wants you and this is how you repay her interest?'

I looked at Andy for a long moment before answering, 'I became a Christian about two months ago.'

I don't know why I told him that. Maybe I was just curious about his reaction to the news. Rhodenburg had dormant anti-discriminatory policies that were activated at the first sign of any employer displaying religious tendencies. They liked their employees to be as non-conformist as possible because it encouraged the free flow of ideas. That was the official line. Not that anyone had ever fallen for it.

It wasn't as if I was actively doing churchy stuff. I accompanied my wife and son to church religiously every Sunday these days because it was what she wanted. I enjoyed the singing, but the excited chatter they called tongues seemed like a whole lot of noise to me. And as for the raising of hands during the singing – worship, I mean – well, I just stood awkwardly and sat down in relief when it was all over. I quite liked the sermons though, even if they made me rather uncomfortable sometimes. Michael had a way of speaking that sometimes made me think that he was talking directly to me. When that happened, I looked very hard at an unseen point above his head and resolved to take up the issue personally with him when I saw him later in the week, which I did. He always insisted that he was merely 'God's mouthpiece' and that if I was 'convicted' by his sermons, then I should 'look into my heart and see what God would like to change and use for his glory.' When he started going off on his churchspeak, I drifted off and started thinking of my 'to do' list.

In the meantime, Kemi and I were reading the daily Bible verses – sometimes together and sometimes even discussing them. That is, when we could; when Yanis *allowed* us the luxury. I also had regular 'guy' meetings with Mark and Pastor Michael. I liked those meetings. We talked about stuff; marriage, the Bible, life... wives! I liked the meetings because there were only the three of us. They gave me a chance to ask questions and, above all, to just be.

Having let loose my confession in the office, Andy was quiet for a moment, then turned away to his desk.

Two slips about my private life in a week. I always kept my private life intensely private. I had told Richard about the children's home on my wedding day as I was waiting for Kemi at the registry office. My exact words to him had been, 'If only the people at the children's home could see me now.' It was a moment of weakness and one I regretted.

It was only a matter of time before this latest slip about my 'getting religion' hit the office grapevine. I lowered my head into my hands, feeling a sick feeling in the pit of my stomach.

'Zachary Kariba, you're a pretty strange fellow.' Andy was shaking his head as he sat down at his desk.

I forced myself to give him a little smile.

'I've worked with you for four years and I *still* don't know anything about you. I knew that you had a girlfriend called Kemi whom you were absolutely crazy about. But I didn't even know you were getting married till it was all over! And then, in one day, in the space of ten minutes, I find out you're a religious fanatic who was raised in a children's home.'

'Funny thing, life,' I said, hoping he would get the hint and leave me alone. I needed to think.

'Yes, very funny.'

My mobile rang again. It was Pastor Michael reminding me that tonight was our regular get-together.

'And you're not allowed to cancel,' he said, laughing.

As if I would. Those weekly get-togethers had become a lifeline.

There was a lot to think about. The meeting with the director of the children's home was in two days. Working on preparation for Liberia was pretty challenging. Then there was Kemi and her career and Yanis. I thought of Kemi and our 'talk' tonight. I knew she wanted to talk about her going back to work. I didn't relish the thought of telling her I was off to Liberia in three weeks. With Andy. And Maxine. Or 'husband stealer' as Kemi liked to call her.

But now Kemi would just have to wait another day.

'Wouldn't dream of missing it,' I replied.

I texted Kemi and told her I was going to the pastor's tonight. She wouldn't mind. It was church stuff. I would be learning about the faith, so she would be happy. Mentally, I prepared myself for a frosty reception when I got home.

6

Mark opened the door, his usual beatific smile on his face. He motioned me to come in. I spotted the pastor in the kitchen. He was getting out plates and cutlery.

'Chinese tonight.'

As if on cue, the doorbell rang behind me. It was our Chinese takeaway. We ate mainly in silence, in the background the television flickering with the latest in Christian television: a black American working up a storm in Pentecostal preaching.

'So noisy.'

Mark and Michael laughed. I hadn't realised I had spoken out loud.

'It's what we call the *anointing*,' Michael said.

'What's that?'

'It's like an enabling from God that equips you to do what he's called you to do.'

'And you have to shout to do that?'

Mark and Michael smiled at each other before both replying, 'Yes!'

I debated for a while before telling them about the Liberia trip. I'd decided to keep the meeting at the children's home to myself. These men knew so much about my life already. I wanted to keep something of my soul to myself. Sometimes I felt like I'd opened up far too much of myself to them and, other times, I was just glad to have people around me I could trust and be myself with. It was a change for me, a loner by nature.

Mark brought out a book and held it towards me. *Answers to Tough Questions about the Christian Faith.*

'You wanted to know where the Bible came from. It's in there. You wanted to know if God existed. It's in there. You wanted to know what would happen to those who had never heard the gospel. It's in there.'

'You've explained all this to me already,' I said, taking the book from him.

'I know. And if I remember correctly, you also said our reasoning defied logic, so here it is. A logical explanation of the gospel by a man of equal intellect as your fine self, one Josh McDowell.'

Pastor Michael held out another book towards me. *Mere Christianity* by CS Lewis.

'And this – by an Oxford lecturer and contemporary of JR Tolkien, no less.'

'I'm honoured.' I gave a mock bow. 'I had no idea you regarded me as someone of such high intellect. I suppose you would like an active discussion on those books?'

'Naturally. When you're done with them. Perhaps you'll be able to tell us something new that lesser mortals like myself and Mark have missed,' he replied. But he said it with a smile.

'How's Vanessa?' I asked Mark.

Mark beamed. 'Fine. Fine. Really enjoying her new job as an office manager. You should see her office prayer list. She goes prayer walking round her office building every Monday at 7.30am.'

I nodded. That sounded very much like Vanessa. Although she was my wife's best friend, they were like fire and water. Vanessa's quiet faith underpinned everything she did, while Kemi's was very much like her personality: fiery red today, arctic tomorrow.

I was curious about one thing, though. 'Do you guys ever argue?'

'Vanessa and me? Not really. It's just not our way.'

'Wow!' I said.

'I know. We're just not wired like that,' he replied.

I fell silent. I was thinking of Kemi and the scheduled talk that I had evaded. I felt rather guilty.

'What's up, Zack?'

Michael had noted the pensive look on my face.

'Is it the Liberia trip? Your wife and kid will be fine. We'll keep an eye on them.'

'Kemi wants to go back to work and I don't think she should. Zack's barely four months old,' I blurted out.

I continued speaking, trying to figure it out in my head.

'When that woman – you know, the one I told you about – aborted my baby, she said that deep down I wasn't as liberal as I thought as I was. It's true. I like having my wife and son home when I come back from work. I like providing for them. They give me purpose. I know it's a sort of out-of-date caveman instinct but I'm also thinking of what's best for Yanis. I do not think a nursery or a nanny can ever replace the care that a mother can give to her child. Maybe, because I grew up in a home, I'm clinging on to an ideal that doesn't exist. But I don't think so. I'm also thinking something else, that maybe Kemi just doesn't want to be with Yanis. After all, she did try to abort him, didn't she?'

I dared not look at the two of them although I knew they wouldn't judge me. In fact, the more time I spent with these two men, the more I respected them. I hadn't realised how busy church ministers were until I started meeting with these two. Mark was Michael's personal assistant and a trainee minister. Even at home, their phones rang continually. The demands on their time were endless yet they made time for me every week without fail; talking to me about Jesus, rugby, football, wives and children. Michael had three children. I knew Mark and Vanessa were keen to start a family but weren't having much success. Mark had made allusions to it but didn't discuss it in much detail. I wondered if Kemi knew. Vanessa probably wouldn't tell her. She was a rather private person.

Now Michael drew in a deep breath.

'Steady on, Zack. Those are wild accusations. Families have been destroyed over far less. Kemi loves that boy. You know she does. Have you tried talking to her about how you feel?'

'No. Every time she brings it up, I shut down. It's like I don't want to face it. There's other stuff as well. The December wedding, moving house, this bid... I mean, if we're both working – and you know how crazy her workload was before she took maternity leave – how's all that going to get done?'

'When we had our first child, Janice went back to work after six months but she felt so guilty at being a working mother that she gave it up. Now we have three children. The children are a bit older now. The youngest is five, so it's not as difficult as it was. Those early years were tough on all fronts – financially, emotionally and all the rest of it – because Janice really struggled with the thought of being at home "doing nothing". Yet she couldn't really go back to work with three children as the childcare costs would've been astronomical. Now, she works from home. She runs a typing service which has really taken off in the last year. You'll be surprised at how many people lack computer skills... Well, my point is, I understand where Kemi is coming from. Janice is not a high-flyer like your wife, but her desire to be validated outside the home is still the same as Kemi's. What say we pray and ask God what he thinks about all this?'

'I think your God has better things to do than listen to a petty little situation between a man and his wife,' I said.

Mark leapt into the conversation.

'You see, that's where you're wrong. God is interested in every area of our lives and if you have a *petty little situation* with your wife, then it's a petty little thing for God to provide answers that will meet you where you are. And he is *your* God as well as mine. When you prayed the sinner's prayer, he also became your God.'

I wasn't convinced but figured I had nothing to lose. Besides, these guys had been there for my Kemi and me, so it seemed almost rude to refuse their genuine request. I wondered why they bothered with me. All I ever seemed to do was poke holes in their faith. Or try to. I looked at my watch. It was 9pm. Kemi would murder me for leaving her alone all day with Yanis.

They both stood up looking solemn.

'Let's pray,' Mark said.

He said a short prayer asking God to reveal his purposes for Kemi and me 'in this situation'. I shuffled. I was still uncomfortable when they prayed. Perhaps it was the ease with which they bared their souls to an invisible being. Or maybe it was the expectation they had that their prayers were being heard and would indeed be answered. I mumbled 'Amen' when Mark finished, said goodnight and left.

When I got home, Kemi gave me the silent treatment. I figured it wasn't the time to tell her about going to Liberia. It would only make things worse.

The next morning as I was buttoning my shirt, she came up behind me, threw her arms around me and planted a kiss on my back.

'I hate it when we argue,' she said.

'So do I. I'm sorry for acting like a jerk yesterday.'

'It's okay. Don't stay too long at the office tonight. Mum and dad will be baby-sitting Yanis for a few hours.'

I turned around and she helped me with my tie.

'My handsome rock.'

'My shining star.'

Yanis let out an almighty cry. We both laughed.

7

Save West Africa was based in a tiny office in Angel. The director used to be a trader in the City. Her name was Helen.

'I left eighteen months ago. Packed it all up because I was miserable. One June morning, I woke up and got ready for work. When I left my flat, it was six o'clock in the morning. I got back to my flat at 10 o'clock. I'd worked a 13-hour day without stopping to eat or even step outside to get some fresh air. My fridge was bare because I didn't have time to shop for groceries. Anyway, I was hardly ever home so there was no point in buying stuff. I had a flat which was in reality a showroom when, deep down, what I dreamed about was having a derelict house that I could do up myself. I hadn't seen my family and friends in weeks and months because I was always working. But that night, when I got home, I sat down, looked around my showy flat and wrote a short letter to my boss. It simply said, "I quit." I gave it to him the next day. Within 30 minutes, my desk had been cleared and I was escorted off the premises.'

I wasn't surprised at that. It was the way of the City.

'When I left the building,' Helen continued, 'I made my way to Waterloo station and caught the next train to Woking where my parents live and spent the next month there. Then I spent a year backpacking around Africa using the proceeds from the sale of my showroom flat. Eventually I settled in Ghana where one of my old school friends lived. I was quite happy there, not doing anything very much, but I knew I couldn't stay there for ever.

'I had to figure out what to do for the rest of my life. My friend in Ghana runs a cooperative for women. The co-op wasn't making enough money and the usual sources of funds, national and international, just weren't enough. Too much competition from other organisations. I thought of my old workplace. I knew they had a CSR – corporate social responsibility policy – even though nothing much was done about it.'

Helen looked at us a little slyly when she said that. I met her eyes head on. Maxine gave her a forced smile, while Andy familiarised himself with the African posters on the walls.

Helen continued, confident her point had been taken. 'So I made them an offer they couldn't refuse. I guaranteed them positive press coverage in the national papers if they donated money. I neglected to mention that my sister was a journalist. But not only that, I offered them something no other charity had ever offered them before.'

She paused, a smile on her face.

'I offered them *The West African Experience*. City traders are very vain and competitive people. They also suffer from burnout. So, instead of stints at rehab clinics, spas, alternative therapy centres or retreats, I offered them Africa. You know... the whole 'helping the people help themselves' thing. They come to Ghana and live as the Ghanaian co-op people live – waking up early, going to work on the farm, and so on. Those that have families bring them; their children go to the local schools along with the African children. The whole emphasis is on experiencing Africa the way its majority experience it.

'My ex-employer bought it. So did their employees. It wasn't their donations that made the papers in the UK, it was my unique way of using *The West African Experience* to bring healing to corporate execs. The scheme worked because every employee that came went back to their jobs more fulfilled. Most of them become regular individual donors.'

We waited for Helen, quite animated now, to take a breath and go on.

'You're wondering why I'm telling you this story. Simple. I came back to the UK three months ago convinced that traditional methods of fundraising need to be changed. There are too many charities competing for the same funds from the same measly donors. And since 9/11 it's become even more difficult. Donors want to fund charities doing stuff in Islam to bolster anti-terrorism. Nobody wants to talk about the real issues facing Africans: poverty, HIV and God-knows-what-else. So imagine my delight when I read your profile and your bid for economic glory in Liberia. I know your CSR is non-existent. I know you came here intending to give me some PR spin about doing good in Liberia and eventually fobbing me off – but that's not going to happen!

'The fact is that your bank needs an organisation like mine on a bid like this. We are your *caring face*. And the fact that you're here shows how desperate you are. Stuff like this is usually done in private. But not this bid. I had wind of it from our Liberia source.'

Helen folded her arms on the table.

'This bid can and will transform lives in Liberia. But only if it's done with that intent. As countries go, Liberia's not as well known as Nigeria or Ghana. Perhaps that's why it's been allowed to go to the dogs. But not any more.'

She stood up and walked resolutely to the door, gesturing us to follow her.

'Thanks for coming in today. It's been a pleasure meeting you. I'll be in touch. Good day.'

It all happened so fast we didn't realise quite what was going on until we found ourselves outside the building.

'What is she on?' Maxine was annoyed. She made as if to go back into the building but Andy stopped her.

'Oldest trick in the book,' he said. 'She was telling us that *Save West Africa* intended to play an active role in the bid whether we liked it or not. We'll see what Richard has to say about that.'

Maxine was muttering under her breath. Andy grabbed her arm.

'Leave it for today. Let's have an early lunch. I'm starving.'

We headed for the Pizza Express opposite the building. I didn't eat much. Not only had Helen given me a lot to think about, but the meeting at the children's home loomed closer. I'd been trying not to think about how I would be affected by going back to the home with all its memories, but still there was something tight lodged in the pit of my stomach. Would any of the staff recognise me? *Dear Lord, let everything go okay tomorrow. Help me to find my mother,* I prayed silently. Funny. It didn't occur to me until later that I was praying in much the same way Mark and Michael did the night before; with hope and without reservation.

Maxine put her hand lightly on my arm. 'Are you okay? You look rather faint.'

I moved my arm away. Her hand fell lamely by her side. Andy pretended he hadn't seen anything, burying himself in his bruschetta.

'I'm fine. Lack of sleep. Yanis does a fine job of keeping us awake.'

She nodded and picked up her fork.

'This project is turning out to be quite something, isn't it?' she said to no one in particular.

'The more I hear about this Liberia place, the more I'm disinclined towards it and as for that Helen woman... perhaps it's just as well I know how to fight as dirty as the best of them.' She bit savagely into a cherry tomato.

I felt more philosophical.

'The fact is, we need her and she knows it. If we have *Save West Africa* on board, it shows our caring side; that we're not just some cowboy investment company going in there and wreaking havoc. *Save West Africa* gives us a heart. And she knows it. Still, her *West African Experience* was a good idea, eh? In fact, I think Rhodenburg could benefit from something like it in all the continents we operate in.'

'We're not a charity,' interrupted Maxine. 'We're going in there to make an impact and create new markets for Rhodenburg. When I'm burned out, I think a few days at a health spa more likely to do the trick than a stint of farm work in Africa singing *Kumbaya*.'

'It's true that the tactics that worked for us in Asia are not going to work for us in Africa,' said Andy.

He grinned. 'It's a whole new ball game. Ask Mr Geldof, he should know. And as for the *Kumbaya* factor, I think it's something we can work in, should we sign up for *The West African Experience.*'

8

Kemi was wearing a dress I hadn't seen before, something black and sparkly that made full use of her new post-Yanis curves. She looked delectable.

'Wow!' I said.

'You like?' she said smiling coquettishly, helping me out of my jacket.

'Me like very much!'

I reached out and pulled her towards me, making growling noises. She slapped my hands lightly.

'Dinner's ready.'

And so it was. My wife had laid out a spread fit for a king. We ate, laughed and flirted with each other. My heart warmed. Everything would work out tomorrow at the children's home. And if it didn't, it didn't matter. Because when it came down to it, this was what really mattered. Family. And I had mine. As desperate as I was to find my parents, I realised that all I was, everything I had, was wrapped in my wife and son. As long as they were okay, then I was okay.

He is before all things, and in him all things hold together.

It was today's Bible verse. I had read it this morning on my way to work but it hadn't made much sense to me then. But hearing it resounding in my heart and being, all of a sudden it did make some kind of sense to me. I had my wife, my son, my job – and my life and everything in it was somehow connected to this burgeoning (and sometimes reluctant) faith of mine...

and this Jesus person I'd been reading about, yet had difficulty grasping. But tonight, in the middle of dinner with my curvaceous wife, hearing those words resounding all through my being confirmed what Michael had told me several times but I hadn't believed: *One day, when you least expect it, those verses will come to you when you need them the most. That's God, talking to you through his word and the Holy Spirit.* Michael was right. Tonight was a penny-dropping night. I understood in that moment more about who Jesus was; I saw that he was the glue that held everything together.

I tried to tell Kemi what I was thinking.

'For the first time, maybe I understand what you mean when you say God talks to you through the Bible.'

'I'm glad.'

I saw her hesitation and touched her arm reassuringly.

'What is it?' I asked gently.

'Zack, I *have* to go back to work. I *need* to go back to work. World Star Baby is scheduled to be broadcast in six months. It's my campaign and I'm sitting at home playing house.'

'You're a mother with a baby. Since when did that translate into *playing* house?'

My voice had become tight. It was no longer flirtatious. The Jesus euphoria that filled me just a few moments before had lifted.

'I'm also a woman with a career to think about.'

'It's not a bad career in itself, being a stay-at-home mother.'

'You would say that, wouldn't you? You get to leave this house every morning. I have to think three times before stepping out of the front door because I have to weigh up my need to go out against the cost of walking round with a buggy that's always in everyone's way loaded with baby supplies!'

She slammed her palm down on the table.

'I should've known that it would be impossible to have a healthy discussion about it with you.'

I wasn't going to let her get away with that.

'That's because you know what you're like deep down inside. You never really wanted Yanis.'

'I see we're back to that again. Go on! You always throw that in my face every time I try to talk to you about stuff that concerns us.'

'I'm trying to get you to see past what *you* want so you can see other people's needs.'

'Well, I'm sorry Mr I'm-so-perfect for not fulfilling your fantasy about hearth and home... '

'Here we go again. Aren't you tired of blowing that particular horn?'

'Obviously not. And you know what? We can talk about this all you want but I'm going back to work. How would you feel if Andy got the legal director position after all the hard work you're doing? Because that's exactly what Sharronne will do to me and my job if I don't get back in there.'

I ignored her jibe about Andy. Kemi had a doctorate in emotional blackmail.

'So while you're working, our son will be in the care of a... a nursery assistant... a stranger.'

I pushed my chair back and stood up, angry. She was doing this to hurt me. I knew she was.

'A qualified person. Somebody who actually knows what they're doing.'

'We're doing okay. We're getting into a routine.'

'*You* may be doing okay. I'm not. Do you know what it's like to stay home, day after day, with a baby latched onto your breast? And you don't make it easy. I still remember what you told me when I couldn't breastfeed Yanis T at first. You said, *I wasn't trying hard enough.* I suppose that's it really. You don't think I try hard enough because, if I did, I wouldn't struggle so much. Look, I wasn't there when that woman took your baby and I am sorry for making you live through that horror again last year. I'm glad I didn't eventually go through with the abortion. I'm sorry, really sorry, so stop punishing me for it. You might not realise it but that is what you're doing. You see these walls?'

She patted the wall behind her. 'They're closing in on me. I need to get out.'

I laid my hands flat on the table and ordered my pounding heart and the roaring in my ears to stop.

'So what are you planning to do?' I asked her quietly.

'I've done it already. I start work in two weeks. *World Star Baby* is on air in six months. It's my campaign and something I'm proud of. I won't let Sharronne steal it from me.'

She sighed heavily. 'Perhaps I'm just not the Mother Earth type.' She got up and started stacking the dishes.

Once Kemi went back to work, I knew there was no way she would come back to being a full-time mother. Not as long as she headed up the *Singing Diapers Star Baby* account.

'Can we at least pray or even talk to Michael about this?' I added, a desperate man clutching at straws.

'You wanted me to have this baby. I did. I made a promise to God that I would love him. I do but... but it's not enough for me. You know that. I'm not like my mother. I'm not Vanessa.'

She sat down heavily, slumping against the table.

'Maybe there's something wrong with me. I thought I could do it... the mother thing... but there are times I resent him so much... '

She was being a martyr again. I couldn't stand it. Couldn't she see it was not about her but about Yanis? I tried another tactic.

'What about God and church?'

'What's that got to do with anything?' she asked coolly.

'You heard me.'

'I see. You've been a Christian for five minutes and all of a sudden you're the expert on *God and church*? How dare you!'

She stormed out of the room.

* * *

'That's serious,' Mark said, when I finished telling him about the scene with Kemi.

I called him and arranged to meet for lunch as soon as I got in to work the next morning.

'You shouldn't have challenged her on her faith like that,' he added.

'But it's true, isn't it? Isn't that what Christian wives should be like? Supportive, nurturing—'

'Do you mean timid, docile housewives at the beck and call of their husbands?'

I started to nod, then stopped abruptly. I knew that if Kemi had been timid and docile, I wouldn't have fallen in love with her. It was her vivacity that drew me to her when we first met.

'Hold on a minute—' I began.

'I'm glad you figured it out yourself. If you wanted a doormat for a wife, then the Church is the wrong place to look.'

Mark took out his Bible and laid it on the café table. Usually, since Mark was rather prone to do this in public places, I would look around in embarrassment to see if anyone was watching. But not now. I wanted to know what the Bible had to say on this latest confrontation between Kemi and me.

'Look here!'

He pointed to a page in his Bible.

'I would like you to read Proverbs 31. I know it's your lunchtime and you have very little time, so just have a quick skim now and read it in more depth later.

'And then... '

His hands went to another part of the Bible and he folded the corner down.

'Read this: 1 Corinthians 7:3 and 4. And, oh yeah, this as well.'

His hands did a quick flip of the pages and he folded the edge of another page.

'Ephesians 5:22 to 33, although I think you probably want to talk about that with your wife.'

I skimmed through Proverbs 31. It was about a business-woman who was full of wisdom and had a grateful husband. I quickly went to 1 Corinthians 7. It was about bodies. What? Time was running out. I had to get back to the office. I flipped to Ephesians and my eyes fell upon a verse: *Husbands, love your wives*...

'Hey, I didn't say I didn't love her,' I said.

'I know,' Mark said, getting up and putting on his jacket.

'Perhaps after work, you should pop back here to Aroma for a bit of time to read those Bible verses again before you go home. I think you will be very surprised at what you'll find. Let me know how it goes.'

'That's it?'

'God's Word is very powerful. He has something to say to you. The question is, are you willing to listen and obey?'

'That's it?'

'That's it.'

Mark bent over and scribbled the verses on a piece of paper. He passed the paper to me. I took it from him politely.

'Call me,' he said, heading towards the café door.

'Sure,' I muttered.

After work, I made my way back to the Aroma, a few minutes walk away from my office, and headed straight for the most secluded table I could find. I ordered a hot chocolate and started reading. At first, I skimmed through the verses; then I decided I was being silly so went back and read them again. This time, I made sure I read the study notes written at the bottom of the pages. Still perplexed, I read them again. Then I sat for a while, just thinking.

I didn't call Mark.

9

A poor man is shunned by all his relatives – how much more do his friends avoid him! Though he pursues them with pleading, they are nowhere to be found (Proverbs 19:7).

That morning I put the devotional booklet back under the pillow. It wasn't what I needed. I wanted something strong and uplifting, not this. The words seemed to mock my current state of confusion.

Arriving at the home, I followed someone called Mary, who met me at reception. I struggled to take in the dramatic changes that had happened in the 12 years since I left. The place had changed almost beyond recognition. The harsh white walls were gone, replaced with wallpapers depicting sunny skies, furry animals and fun shapes. It was a sea of yellows, blues and reds. The smells were the same though: over-boiled cabbage and bleach.

I was 15 years old before I finally realised that I wasn't wanted. I wasn't going to be adopted. I wasn't going anywhere. I was a young adult. Foster and adoptive parents wanted cute little babies and children with as few complications as possible. Teenagers were regarded as too much work, with already-formed personalities. So, at 15, I faced some harsh realities: the children's home was my home, the staff and other children my family. Once I reconciled myself to these facts, life was easier. I stopped trying hard to be loved. I crushed every fantasy I had of my tearful, remorseful parents coming to the home to 'rescue' me. I concluded that life in the home wasn't at all bad; it could've been worse. I knew others that were, in fact, a lot worse.

Finally, I made some decisions about how I wanted my life to be and took steps to ensure that it would turn out that way. I already knew I wanted to be a lawyer. I knew I didn't want to be financially dependent on anyone. I also knew that people that worked in the City of London were rich. So I concluded that I would be a lawyer who worked in the City.

During my first year with the law firm that sponsored my law degree, I decided I wanted to be a corporate lawyer. It didn't take me long to change focus that little bit. The terms of my law scholarship dictated that I worked at the donor law firm for at least two years after graduation. I served the terms and handed in my resignation the exact date the tenure ended. After that, I worked as a junior legal adviser for a small investment house for two years while studying for my bar exams. Shortly after, I ended up at Rhodenburg as a senior legal adviser. I had my eyes fixed on being Legal Director: Africa. Uncharted territory but a post in which I knew I could make my mark.

Mary was still walking and I followed, lost in memories. We passed the dining hall. The dark, heavy benches and tables had been replaced by light, contemporary furniture. The walls were hung with paintings that had obviously been done by the kids themselves. I had been anxious to avoid bumping into any staff member who might recognise me, but I need not have bothered. All the staff looked to be under 35. I knew without being told that these staff members had twenty-first century psychology degrees or diplomas in social policy.

We stopped at the door to the director's office and Mary motioned me to go in. There he was – the man with the keys to my past and future.

'Come in, come in,' he said, waving me into the office.

He was around 40, no more, with thinning hair and a warm, genuine smile. I felt the tension ease a little as I shook his hand. *God, I hope he knows what he's doing. Isn't he rather too young to be the director of a children's home?*

I sat down, feeling unsure, insignificant. I tried to shut out yesterday's events. Things had not improved between Kemi and me when I got home. We didn't talk. I played with Yanis in the bedroom while Kemi pottered about in the kitchen. I wanted to tell her about the verses I'd read. I wanted to apologise to her, but the words stuck in my throat.

So... a young director. What could he know about running a children's home? He probably had a degree in alternative therapy.

'Pleasure to meet you, Zack. Tea, coffee?'

I declined. I wanted to run. The mission was over. I wanted to go home to my son, hold him, smell him and touch him. I didn't want to be here with this man telling me stuff about my life that I didn't want to hear.

'Call me Tristan.'

I didn't want the pleasantries. 'You're going to be able to help me, aren't you?' I asked, pointedly.

'I'm afraid it's not quite as easy as that. You're a lawyer so you understand that there are legalities one has to follow for the sake of both parties. It's not a question of wanting or not wanting to help you, more a question of ensuring that we do not break laws intended to protect those that need protecting in situations like this. There are three parties involved here: the home, yourself and perhaps the individuals that might be able to help us. I have to think of what's legally best for everyone.'

I didn't reply. I got up and went to the window. There were children in the playground. A football match of sorts was going on. Some of the older children were reading on a bench.

'Not quite the same as in your day, is it?' Tristan said, watching my face.

'No. For one thing, you have fewer children now.' I moved away from the window and returned to the seat across from his desk.

'There are only 50 children in the home now. In your time there must've been, what? About 80? What was it like?'

I shrugged. 'It wasn't Oliver Twist. I suppose it could've been worse.'

'I see you're married.'

He had spotted the ring on my finger.

'Any kids?'

'Yes, Yanis. He's almost 18 weeks.' *And too young to be abandoned by his parents in a nursery.*

'Mary and I couldn't have children – but this has more than made up for it. It's hard work though,' he smiled.

I didn't smile back and disliked myself for it. I just wanted what I came here for so that I could leave. I wished Kemi was with me, telling me that the Lord was with me and that everything would be okay. Perhaps I didn't need her to tell me that. Perhaps it was time I started believing it for myself. Perhaps it was time I realised that I still didn't really know the woman I had married.

'So... what?' I asked Tristan, forcing my mind to the situation at hand.

'What can you tell me?'

'Pretty much all I have is what you already know, I suspect. Someone left you outside this home when you were about 48 hours old. A tour of the local hospitals produced nothing, which suggests that you were born at home or maybe without medical supervision. The staff who were here the night you were found have either died, moved abroad or are simply not to be found. Looking at the records, I see that when you left this place 12 years ago you made it clear that you didn't want to be contacted by anyone from the home. Quite understandable. Some people do that. Starting afresh.'

Tristan glanced down at a slim folder of papers on his desk.

'I've made a few calls for you and the only person that remembers you, or should I say, we could trace, is the gardener. He retired about five years ago and he still lives in London. I haven't been able to speak to him because apparently he's in Wales on holiday. But I've left a couple of messages with his neighbours for him to contact me, and sent him a letter. He doesn't have a mobile. I can't give you his details because of the Data Protection Act, but if you give me a call in a fortnight I might have some news for you. If he's willing, of course.'

'His name was Jack. Jack Morris,' I said.

I remembered him well. There were other things I was remembering even though I didn't want to. The day I left the home I was determined to cut off all links with my past because I wanted a new beginning. Not a past that clung to me like graveclothes. Sure, the staff had taken care of me as best they could with limited resources. I knew I had repaid them badly by deleting them from my memory bank. It wasn't a comfortable feeling. Was that how my mother had felt as she abandoned me? That I was her past and she wanted to move into a baggage-free future?

'Yes. That's his name.' Tristan held out his hands. 'He's the only lead I've got.'

I held out my hand and shook his. 'Thank you. I appreciate your help.'

10

I left The Florence Nightingale Children's Home intending to head straight home to my son. Instead, I found myself at my in-laws' house. Gail was home on her own. This woman, my wife's mother, loved me as if I was her own son. She had fought for Yanis' life with me when Kemi had wanted to abort him.

The house was filled with the smell of jollof rice and mixed meat. I inhaled the scent. Gail had cooking Nigerian-style down to a fine art. I wished Kemi excelled in the same way. She was good at cleaning, though. Or had been, before Yanis.

'Hey! I've just put aside some food packages for you guys. And hasn't my grandson grown! I called by two days ago. He looks like a little frog!'

I made all the right noises while Gail nattered on. She wasn't fooled. She knew I wasn't listening.

'Talk to me.' She patted the space on the sofa next to her.

'I don't know what to say, Gail. Things are just not working out the way I thought they would.'

'I know. Kemi called her dad last night.'

I wished she hadn't done that. I was her husband. She should run to me in times of crisis, not to her father. But I might have guessed it. She was his little princess. Gail, in contrast, was the disciplinarian. Kemi called her 'the virago' – more than a little unfair.

'Be patient. It takes longer for some women to come to terms with the whole motherhood thing. Being responsible for a child doesn't always come easily. Remember, Kemi is our only child. No siblings. She's never been responsible for anyone except herself. You were raised in a home. You had responsibilities for yourself and others when you were there. There's a big difference.'

'Gail, she wants to go back to work,' I blurted out, thumping one fist into the sofa arm.

'She wants to put our son, who's still breastfed, into the care of a nursery assistant because of this advertising campaign for *World Star Baby*. I just wish she would discuss it properly. But no! She's made the decision without talking to me first.'

'Like it would've made a difference? Don't kid yourself! You know you would've said no to her going back to work. Deep inside, you're the original caveman. Everybody seems to know this but you.

'In any case, it's *her* job. Why should she feel less passionately about her job than you do about yours? At work, she's in her element. She knows what she's doing. Parenting... well, that's another thing entirely. She's adrift in the unknown, making it up as she goes along, hoping for the best.'

Gail shrugged and gave me a hard stare.

'Well, I hear you've got religion yourself now. The extra help from on high will come in handy for both of you.'

I decided to ignored this last bit. She didn't get it. I couldn't expect her to. It wasn't a matter of 'getting religion'. I was beginning to see it was something bigger, deeper and infinitely more fulfilling... I still had a lot of figuring out to do in my head. This wasn't the time to take Gail on.

'It's not about the job. Don't you see? She doesn't want Yanis. Every time she looks at him, she blames me for making her have a baby against her will. She would rather be doing something else. Anything else.'

'Oh, put a sock in it! She loves Yanis to bits! She just can't cope with him. There's a difference. And I think you should stop before you say something you'll regret. Kemi's had a tough year. Possible abortion, promotion, childbirth, wedding, parenting... She's trying hard to adjust to life not lived on just

her own terms but according to the needs of someone else –
namely Yanis Woboluwamitito. And you should be patient. It's
not easy being cooped up in a tiny flat with a baby. It's hard
work. My daughter is not a nestler. We both know that. We just
hoped that Yanis would tame her. Give her some time. She'll
come round, you'll see.'

*Give her some time... It's not easy being cooped up in a tiny
flat with a baby.* No one was listening to me. Not Michael. Not
Mark – and certainly not Gail. I knew what I was talking about.
I knew Kemi resented Yanis. I tried another approach.

'I'm doing my best. I'm putting the flat on the market and I'm
looking at some houses later this week.'

Well, that was the plan. But would we still be together as a
family by the time I found a new home?

And what about Jack Morris? Where did he fit into all this?

I could hear Pastor Michael's voice. *Remember Zack. One day
at a time. That's how life is lived. Not much point in getting
ahead of God.*

I wanted to tell Gail about Jack but stopped myself in time.
She would dissuade me. *You have enough on your plate with
your son and Kemi. Why go looking for trouble?*

I tore my mind away from its wandering thoughts and focused
on the present.

'How's Foluke?'

'Someone needs to speak some sense into that girl. She's
actually intent on marrying that bloke she met on the
Internet.'

Foluke was my wife's cousin on her father's side. She
decamped to Nigeria six months ago after an online romance
with a man living there.

'Maybe it's true love?'

Gail's look said otherwise.

'Maybe you should shut your mouth! Femi is up in arms about
the whole thing. Foluke's his favourite niece. Foluke's father is
also up in arms. He wants Femi to go to Nigeria and speak to
Foluke, perhaps even meet the said bloke. They say he's a
gold digger.' She spat out the last sentence.

'I'm passing through Lagos soon myself.'

'Well, then! That's settled! *You* can see Foluke. Bring some sanity to this madness. But what on earth are you going to be doing in Lagos?'

I told her about work and Liberia. I neglected to mention that I hadn't told my wife about the trip yet. If she was serious about going back to work in two weeks, it would be the same time as I was going to Liberia.

This wasn't the kind of life I had ever envisioned for my son. I wanted him in a loving, secure home, cared for by committed parents – not the kind that carted him off to nursery because their careers were more important. And something else was starting to bug me: was I displaying the same tendencies as my own parents? OK, taking Yanis to a nursery or a childminder wasn't on the same scale as abandoning him for good in a children's home... But he was so small.

It was getting late. I left laden with good-smelling food packages. When I got home, the atmosphere was still decidedly frosty. I dumped everything in the fridge, made a sandwich, got ready for bed and picked up Yanis, who was grizzling in his cot. I shook his rattle and talked to him until he fell asleep on my chest. Placing one hand on his back to support him, I picked up my Bible with the other. Then I started reading again the verses Mark gave me yesterday. Later, when Kemi joined us on the bed somewhat hesitantly, I put the Bible aside and drew her to me.

'It's never been my intention to chain you to the kitchen sink. I'm just thinking of Yanis,' I said.

'I love him too, you know. I just can't cope with him all the time,' she replied, lifting the sleeping Yanis off my chest. She put him in his cot and we both waited expectantly for an indignant howl. Nothing came. Just a tiny burp. Kemi came back to the bed. I wrapped my arms around her and felt desire rising within me. She felt it too and responded. Afterwards I told her about Liberia and Foluke. She listened quietly. She didn't even seem bothered when I mentioned that Maxine would be on the trip. Maybe she didn't care. Perhaps she did. But not nearly enough.

'Me going back to work will be okay. I know it will. If it doesn't work out, I'll quit. I promise,' Kemi said.

I told her about reading Proverbs 31. She rolled her eyes.

'That woman does not exist,' she said.

'I thought you said the Bible was infallible?'

'I just think that particular proverb is another mechanism to hold church women to an ideal that doesn't exist.'

'Are you allowed to say that?'

She looked at me questioningly.

'It's not a crime to have an opinion on the Bible,' she said.

'But you've just said that you didn't believe in the Proverbs 31 woman even though you say you believe the Bible is... what is it?... the *inerrant* Word of God.'

'We've just made up. Why are you being so difficult?'

'I'm not. I just want to understand how you could gain such a different understanding of something we've both read.'

Kemi sighed.

'Fine. What did you think the proverb meant?'

I reached out for one of her unruly curls. She slapped my hand away impatiently.

'Talk!'

'Well, when I read it yesterday and today, all I could think about was how you were that woman the Bible was talking about.'

'Me? How do you work that out?'

'Well, it says she's worth more than rubies, she works hard at her cloth business, even gets into wine trading, earns enough to give to the poor. Then there's the bit about her husband having full confidence in her—'

'Oh yeah?' Kemi interrupted.

'Let me finish. When I read that bit, I had this thought... that the reason I didn't want you to go back to work was because you're so good at what you do. Yanis and I will be left behind while you go on to be the queen of advertising.'

I thought she would interrupt me again then but she didn't. She had a strange look on her face. I continued talking.

63

'I realise that maybe I've been not only just a bit jealous but a bit selfish too. I read some stuff in Ephesians and Corinthians. Well, somewhere there it says that husbands should love their wives as they love their own bodies—'

'Zack, you're really freaking me out here!'

'Why? I thought you would be happy about this stuff. Isn't that what you've always wanted? A Christian husband?'

'Well, yes... but now that it's happening, it's just weird. It's a good kind of weird though.'

'Good weird?'

'Yes.' Kemi started rearranging pillows under our heads.

'But there's something else. One of the verses talked about the husband being the head of the wife because Jesus is the head of the Church and he died for the Church. I'll die for you, Kemi, but I'm not your head. I think men and women are equal.'

'Zack, do we have to talk about this now?'

'I'm just saying—'

'Say all you want. You've made me very happy tonight. My handsome rock.'

She drew my arms tightly around her waist and yawned. I closed my eyes, feeling happier than for some time. *Perhaps I should've told her about the children's home.*

11

When I got to work the next day, there was an email message from Richard. Helen would like a meeting at our office.

'I just know she'll want to tag along with us to Liberia,' Maxine said.

And she was right.

More than that. Helen had scheduled meetings for us in Liberia with everyone who was anyone in Monrovia, Liberia's capital. And just to ensure that *Save West Africa* got their share of the bid pie, she had one of her Liberian colleagues enlisted as our guide while we were there.

'Guide? More like spy,' Maxine muttered during the meeting.

Helen heard her and threw a smile in her direction. Richard didn't look our way. He kept nodding at Helen and waited for her to finish.

'You do realise, don't you, that we do not have a contract with *Save West Africa* so we're not legally bound to you,' I told Helen.

'No problem,' she said smoothly. 'I brought something with me.'

She pushed some documents across the table. Richard handed them to me and I flicked through them quickly, summarising for the rest of the team as I scanned through the detail. I was impressed. She knew what she was talking about. It was the kind of contract that made Rhodenburg accountable for all things and *Save West Africa* for nothing.

Helen waited impassively. She knew Rhodenburg would agree. We needed *SWA* for the bid; they were our compassionate face.

'Andy, what's the deal?' Richard was impatient.

Andy drew his chair closer into the table. 'The fact is, we need a caring face for this bid and none of the other charities have come up with the same kind of goods that *SWA* have. I'm looking at this in the long term and I do think that perhaps, after this bid, *SWA* could be our adopted charity.'

Helen was staying cool.

'*Save West Africa* will consider your request. But in the meantime, we need to finalise your Monrovia itinerary. Our contact there knows everyone, so while you're on your official feasibility tour, she'll be assisting you with your *unofficial* feasibility studies. I must warn you that things are not always what they seem out there, so tread carefully. But then, you don't need me to tell you that. After all, you've worked in Asia.'

Maxine bristled and Richard thanked Helen for coming. It was official. *Save West Africa* was our watchdog. It would ensure that in the event we won the bid, we would adhere to international diamond mining and trading standards and, of course, gain ourselves *West African Experiences*.

I could see how Helen had bamboozled her ex-employers into investing in the Ghanaian co-op. I admired her. She was a smooth and consummate professional. It was only a matter of time before she became one of those million-dollar celebrity fundraisers.

I reflected that there was something of Kemi, advertising executive extraordinaire, in her. They were both very determined people.

'Men are so fallible,' Maxine hissed as we left the room. 'One minute we're bidding for a contract and the next, we're saddled with east London's answer to Bob Geldorf. Can someone explain to me what in the world is going on here?'

Andy spoke up, rather sharply, I thought.

'We need *SWA* as much as they need us. Remember East Timor? If we'd had something like *Save West Africa* on our side, we wouldn't have had that run-in with Greenpeace and Human Rights Watch. The East Timor debacle cost us US$100 million. A very expensive mistake. One we're still recovering from. Think about that before you start mouthing off about *Save West Africa.*'

'East Timor cost us because somebody wasn't doing their job properly—'

I stepped in before the two of them declared all-out war on each other.

'I think we should leave it for today. We have a lot to do.'

Maxine glared at me, then turned and strode towards her desk.

'She's jealous. She saw the way you looked at Helen,' Andy said.

'What do you mean? I wasn't *looking* at Helen.'

'Sure you weren't,' Andy replied.

Andy was a pretty easy-going guy and I didn't dislike him. He was just someone I worked with. However, there were times when his over-active imagination grated on my nerves. I wished he would grow up.

* * *

So where was the airport? All I could see was a clearing in the middle of lush jungle. Then I spotted the UN helicopters and aeroplanes. Maxine leaned over me to look out of the window. Irritated, I leaned right into the back of my seat and continued looking aout the window to stop my eyes disappearing into her cleavage.

'Zack, I think that really is the airport. That's Roberts International Airport.' Her voice was a whisper.

It couldn't be. But it was. The airstrip, all two or so miles of it, was littered with aid aircraft and UN helicopters. We stared out at a small, shabby bungalow set amid trees and manned by UN officials.

The Bellview aeroplane taxied to a stop. A coach drove onto the tarmac and steps were put up to the plane. Andy, hot and bothered, was sweating profusely. I doubted Maxine and I looked much better. I longed to go back to Lagos, Nigeria. Eight of my ten-hours stopover there had been spent in the comfortable air-conditioned confines of the Sheraton Hotel.

I hadn't been able to meet up with Foluke there yesterday. I'd called her and she told me she knew the family had sent me to 'knock some sense' into her head but she didn't care. She was going to marry her penniless lover and there was nothing anyone could do about it. I told her I would give her another call when I was en route from Liberia.

The passengers' chatter increased when the plane stopped. They were a mix of Nigerians, aid workers and veteran journalists. The journalists, in particular, had the jaded look of seasoned travellers. I wondered at the horrors they'd seen in their years of war reporting.

I was already missing my wife and child terribly. I wondered how Yanis was coping on his first day at the nursery. Were the nursery assistants feeding him right? I hoped they didn't leave him to cry. I tried to crush the guilt threatening to overwhelm me. Kemi and I were terrible parents doing this to our child. He didn't belong in a nursery, even if it was private. It was small, with a high ratio of staff to children. I didn't want Yanis fighting for the attention of some harassed nursery assistant with ten other children to look after. Kemi protested the expense. I said if she was going to be queen of advertising, we would do the nursery thing my way.

And now here I was in Liberia, West Africa, looking at the ruins of a decrepit bungalow masquerading as an airport terminal, and the comings and goings of some blue-helmeted UN officials. The airport was one of the first places the US marines secured in the 2003 carnage of the civil war. It was a necessary move to guarantee the supplies of aid and reinforcements against the rebels threatening to take control of Monrovia and, eventually, the country. In the end, President Charles Taylor was offered asylum in Nigeria in return for ceasing hostilities. A peace accord which offered leadership positions in the transitional government to rebel leaders, government factions and a few civilians was drawn up and signed in Accra, Ghana.

Maxine, Andy and I were about to enter the bungalow building when two men stepped in front of us and extended their hands towards us. They introduced themselves as Martin and Ben, our security personnel from *SWA*. They shepherded us into a brand new Cherokee Jeep, where we waited while one of them negotiated our luggage. We didn't even go through immigration.

Ben drove with Martin next to him. The three of us in the back were left to absorb the shock of the scenery around us.

Roberts International was stationed some 30 or so miles outside Monrovia, with just one road between it and the capital. To either side was a sea of dark green forest and swamp. We passed little village communities, burnt-out buildings, mission centres and churches. And more churches.

'They warned me about this,' Andy murmured.

Martin looked round and nodded. 'The churches are a powerful force in this country. Liberia was built on traditional Christian values. The first president was a Methodist preacher, I think. Traditionally, successive presidents have been Freemasons while proclaiming some form of adherence to the Baptist denomination. There are other denominations as well but, when the war was officially declared over, almost overnight new Pentecostal churches sprang up. They're mostly run by Nigerians. They have a very strong presence in this sub-region.'

I wondered if I would be able to go to one of the churches in my free time. I wanted to. I berated myself for not asking Michael if he could give me any church contacts in Liberia. I was beginning to look forward to my family's Sunday church outings. I would miss them. Then again, I was here to work and notch up some professional glory, I reminded myself.

We drove for an hour, passing the UN warehouse and training buildings, roadblocks manned by the Nigerian and Ghanaian UN peacekeeping battalion. Occasionally, we passed pedestrians carrying huge bundles of green leaves on their heads, presumably to sell.

'Any green vegetables are just called greens here. During the war, many people lived in these forests and swamps. Not so many now,' Ben said.

Maxine continued looking out of the window. I wondered what she was thinking as we passed young girls no more than 12 years old carrying babies held on their backs with cloth slings. No doubt the babies too were relics of war. We passed scores of sullen, listless young men, many staring after us with bloodshot eyes. Had they participated in the atrocities?

The human traffic increased as we neared the city. At a junction we turned left past several foreign embassies, most of them faded and bullet-ridden bungalows. Martin pointed out the striking Nigerian Embassy, which stood out like Buckingham Palace. A few Nigerian UN peacekeepers were hanging around the building and I noticed the deference with which the Liberians approached them.

Martin shrugged. 'A lot of Nigerian blood has been spilt in West Africa. Wherever there's been a war, it's the ECOWAS troops consisting of Nigerians and to a lesser extent Ghanaians that have fought against rebel groups. You go to Sierra Leone and elsewhere in the region, it's the same. The locals cannot do enough for them.'

I wanted to ask him how he and Ben ended up in Liberia but decided against it. Some things were better not known. They were probably mercenaries who fought in the war and had now turned security experts. One thing was clear: they were at home in Monrovia. I had met people like Ben and Martin on a couple of Rhodenburg jaunts to Sarajevo – a disastrous affair if ever there was one. The endemic corruption had proved to be way too much for any investments to be made. Rhodenburg lost money. Not a lot – a few million.

Our jeep pulled up outside a white building. Urban Villa Hotel, Sinkor was signposted outside. Ben and Martin jumped out and three men came running from the hotel. A generator hummed loudly in the background. I remembered from the FT report that there hadn't been electricity, running water or telephone lines for the last 14 years in the country. How did people *live*?

'Welcome to Monrovia,' the hotel staff greeted us. Their English was a mixture of pidgin, old American South and something else. While they unloaded our luggage, the three of us looked around. Maxine was ominously quiet. Andy led the way into the hotel.

A woman was waiting for us in the cool, air-conditioned confines of the hotel reception. She came towards us, hand extended.

'Hello, I'm Grace, *SWA* Liberia Officer. I hope you had a good flight.'

I froze. It was *that woman*.

12

My steps faltered. I hadn't seen her in eight years. There was hardly a sign of recognition from her. Just the faintest flicker in her eyes. My own eyes swam in mist. Pain washed over me. I felt physically sick, weak. In Africa of all places. Why? And why now?

Trust me.

But I was angry. I wanted to go somewhere I could be alone and bleed emotionally. I blinked and looked at her. She had her hand out towards Andy but she was watching me with a bemused expression. What she was up to? The witch! The impulse to run towards her and do her long-lasting physical damage was overwhelming.

Zack, trust me. I will work it out for your own good. You'll see.

I wished I could ignore the voice. I gathered all my emotional strength to switch off. I wasn't going to listen to the voice. It would make me weak.

Maxine stepped forward.

'Pleased to meet you, Grace.'

'Zack,' I heard myself announce to her. As if she didn't know.

I wandered over to the window while Ben and Martin dealt with the formalities of checking-in and Andy and Maxine made small talk with that woman... Grace. Finally, Grace told us she would be back in a few hours. She suggested we had some sleep and freshen up.

'We have a very busy itinerary. This might be the only time you actually get to see your hotel during the daylight,' she smiled, exposing her fangs. No doubt she'd sunk them into every male within a five-mile radius purely for the purposes of international relations.

I didn't bother waiting for the hotel staff. I picked up my bags and followed the security men. They needed to check our rooms. Apparently, an American had been killed a few weeks before. An intruder had entered his hotel room through the ceiling. His ending was gruesome. A murder suspect was being held in the only jail in the city.

I looked at my watch. 3pm, UK time. The nursery would close in another hour and Kemi would pick up Yanis. I hoped he wouldn't forget me. I couldn't wait to speak to Kemi and hear her voice. She would make me feel better. She would make the spectre of that woman go away.

Who was I kidding? I knew I would never tell Kemi about meeting that woman in Liberia.

I knew that my UK mobile would not work in Liberia so I asked one of the hotel staff if they could get me a Liberian SIM card. The young man nodded and went off. I sat on the bed, head in my hands. What now? I'd never needed Michael or Mark so much. They would know what to do. They always had answers.

My week-long stay in Liberia stretched in front of me like a prison sentence. Out of habit, I recalled the day's Bible verse. I was becoming dependent on these Bible verses, beginning to learn that, if distilled with understanding, even the most obscure verses eventually offered relief. And the more verses I read, the more I was compelled to read. Today's verse was a good one: *The Lord is my shepherd, I shall not be in want.*

There was a knock on my door. I ignored it. Then another louder, more persistent knock and Maxine's voice. 'Zack, it's me. Let me in.'

I'd already noted that her room was directly across the corridor from mine. I rose from the bed, expecting a repeat of last night's performance at the Sheraton. I'd opened my door to find her in barely-there nightwear. I didn't blink. I'd simply shut the door and called my wife in London. Then I called Pastor Michael. By the time I'd finished on the phone with him, it was all I could do to keep awake. Maxine and her nightwear had been deleted from my memory bank by then.

I stood in the doorway, wanting Maxine to get the message loud and clear: *Leave me alone!*

She stood on tiptoe and tried to see into the room by looking over my shoulder.

'What do you want?'

'What's the deal with you and this Grace? I saw the way the two of you looked at each other.'

'Not right now, Maxine. I need to rest.'

I made as if to shut the door. She hesitated for a moment. I felt guilty. Good manners won the battle. Hopefully she wouldn't refer to last night.

'I'm sorry. I guess the heat's getting to me,' I said, uncomfortably.

She tried to step into my room. Still I blocked it. Guilt or not, a man had a right to bleed in private. She looked at me as if she was trying to figure me out. Finally she sighed.

'I was just trying to help,' she said.

With what? Irritated, I repeated that I wanted to nap and freshen up. At that point Andy came out of his room, took in the scene, and then went back inside.

I'd had enough. I shut the door in her face.

Tristan should have heard from Jack Morris now. I'd given him a call before coming to Liberia to let him know I was going to be away. He said he hadn't yet heard from Jack.

* * *

Another knock on my door jerked me awake.

'Mister, I got the SIM card,' a voice said.

I got up and opened the door and took the SIM card from a man who told me his name was Johnny. As I thanked him, Martin came out of his room along the corridor.

He nodded at me. 'We leave in thirty minutes. Remember, don't leave any valuables in your room and your passport must always be on your person. Do you want a quick coffee or tea from the restaurant downstairs?'

'I just need to have a quick shower, make a call and I'll be with you.'

* * *

That woman... Grace... She hadn't changed. Her skin was darker from her exposure to the Liberian sun. I didn't know how long she'd been in the country but, from the way she interacted with the locals, it had been a while. Everyone seemed to know who she was. She waved and said hello to the UN peacekeepers at all the checkpoints.

I'd met her at university. She was a politics and philosophy student and a liberal through and through. She hated people telling her what to do and was loath to explain her actions to anyone. I thought then that she was free-spirited, open-minded. Later I changed my view, believing her brand of open-mindedness was just an excuse to be self-centred.

We dated for a year. We parted because she aborted my baby. Later I found out that she hadn't been faithful the whole time we were together. Now here she was in Monrovia doing God knows what. I didn't know which was worse: the shock of finding her here, the thought of spending the next six days with her, or the anger and pain I felt when I remembered the misery she'd caused me in the past.

I felt hatred well up within me. Her complacent verbal diarrhoea filled up the jeep as she kept up a non-stop commentary, pausing now and again to greet someone on the road. The urge to announce to everyone in the car what she'd done to me was overwhelming.

I felt instinctively that Maxine wouldn't like her. What were the other men making of her?

I concentrated on the heavily potholed roads and surroundings – a riot of colours, smells and activity. So busy! Some people were trying to flag down buses or taxis signed with Bible verses and entreaties to God. Some of the writings were comical to say the least. Like *Praise God – but pay your fares first.*

People were selling goods from trays carefully balanced on their heads. They approached cars in the slow-moving traffic and displayed their wares. The billboards were filled with adverts for alcohol and health warnings about HIV. We passed bullet-ridden buildings and new church buildings proclaiming 'Jesus Christ is King!'

'Zachary... you haven't said much.'

She always did call me Zachary. I hated it. *Help me God*, I prayed silently. I was afraid of what I would do if I couldn't control the whirl of emotions I was experiencing.

'Right now I don't have anything to say. And the name is Zack,' I said.

She smiled tightly. Maxine looked from her to me and then back again.

'So, Grace,' she said, 'What's a nice girl like you doing in a place like Liberia?'

'Nothing very unusual. A woman wakes up one day and decides she doesn't want to settle for the mediocrity of the nine-to-five. She packs her bag and ends up in West Africa, only to find herself in the middle of a civil war. The rest, as they say, is history.'

'But where were you when they were chopping off people's limbs and disembowelling pregnant women?' This from Andy.

Ben answered. 'Grace has the skin of a chameleon. She moves around and somehow blends into the scenery. Sometimes here, sometimes in Sierra Leone, sometimes she pops up in Nigeria.'

'Where trouble is, be certain that there you will find Grace,' Martin quipped.

'Not true!' protested Grace. 'I just like to see things for myself and understand why things happen... and if I can do some good in the process, then so much the better.'

'What good? Putting yourself in dangerous situations just for the sake of it?' Maxine voice had risen.

Grace raised her eyebrows.

'By choosing to stay during the war, I show these people that I identify with them,' she replied.

Martin spoke up.

'When the war broke out, the British consulate tried to forcibly eject Grace from Liberia. She refused. The rebels came to her house. Everyone knew who she was and where she lived. She was running free adult literacy classes in her compound. The night they came for her, she had 50 women and children hiding in various places around her home. None of the 50 people were harmed because Grace decided that she would rather she was raped by these rebels, all ten of them mind – five of whom were drug-crazed teenagers – than let them harm one of the people who sought refuge in her home. They were just about to do the deed when Ben and I came on the scene. Let's just say that we secured the situation.'

Maxine looked down at her hands; the rest of us were silent and still. Grace, looking out of the window, spoke again.

'I'd taught some of those same child soldiers how to read. Some of the children used to go to church children's groups. The boys that came to my house were wearing blond wigs, carrying machine guns and high on whatever they'd been given by their soldier leaders. When things had died down and the UN was in control and the war declared officially over, the boys came back to my house. They said they were sorry. They hadn't wanted to come to my house that night but their commander said that I was a spy for Charles Taylor and that he would kill them if they didn't do what they were told. They were just scared kids.

'The horror of their experiences as child soldiers has terribly scarred them. The war might be over but the old ties to these fiendish leaders still remain and could be resuscitated at any time. That's why we have to ensure that we actively engage these ex-child soldiers in productive work, otherwise... '

Trust her to come across looking like some self-sacrificing do-gooder.

13

Nigerian UN peacekeepers waved us through the gates of an official-looking building to park in a line of similar Jeep Cherokees. Martin said they all belonged to members of the transitional legislature. The jeeps were among the perks of the job, he added.

'We're going to meet Senator Williams: reformed rebel leader, God-fearing man and presidential candidate,' Martin said.

'You forgot to mention his other titles: warlord and arms dealer,' Grace added.

The building had known some former glory but had fallen into disrepair. Senator Williams, jovial and overweight, didn't look much like a warlord. I could see Maxine and Andy thought the same. There were broad smiles and handshakes all around.

In his room, an air conditioner bleated out some little respite from its tired vents. The dark curtains were drawn to shut out any trace of the scorching sun. Chairs were produced as we all crowded into the room. I noticed the senator didn't look at Ben and Martin.

Andy and I faced the big man opposite his table. We whipped out our business cards, exchanged pleasantries and got down to business.

The senator began by telling us how pleased he was by our visit. The world had forgotten about Liberia and he hoped our visit would be one of many.

Then Grace interrupted. Rather rudely, I thought.

'Senator, in view of the reason for our visit, we wondered if you could give us a copy of the mines and banks report so that we could have a clearer perspective of the economic assessment we need to make.'

The senator ignored her. Andy drew himself closer to the table.

'That would be much appreciated, senator,' he said.

Senator Williams drew in a deep breath.

'The report is still being drafted by the appropriate committee. We will get it to you once it's completed.'

Grace broke in again.

'I was told by the World Bank Liberian official that you had already submitted the report to them for consideration.'

'It's a Liberian matter. One of national importance and, as you can imagine, it is not for public consumption.'

The senator glared at her. I could tell they were well acquainted with each other.

'Isn't that why we are all here, for the sake of Liberia? It has been suggested that certain people are not keen to publicise that report because it is thought to be too explosive. I'm sure that you are not one of those people.'

She swept her arm around the room.

'These kind people are here to do some good in this wonderful country and I am sure that you would not like them to go back to the UK empty-handed. That would not speak well of the world-famous Liberian generosity.'

'You can think what you like. The report is not ready. Unfortunately, I have a meeting scheduled in five minutes so you'll have to leave. Charlie will escort you outside the building.'

'It would be a shame if we left this building without that report, particularly as Rhodenburg is not only making an economic assessment but are seeking trained management for their Liberia operations... '

'Save me your patronising rubbish. I don't want to hear it. Charlie!' the senator barked.

A young lad ran into the room.

'Could you make copies of the *draft* Mines report for these people. They'll wait outside for them.'

I noticed that Grace's hands were trembling slightly while we waited in the corridor. Charlie came back with the copies. We all breathed more easily when we got outside.

'Gees, Grace. I told you to be careful!'

'Martin, I'm sorry!'

Grace turned to us.

'Senator Williams is still trading guns and he's currently sending child soldiers to the Congo,' she said.

'So why is he still a senator?' asked Andy.

Martin shrugged. 'The peace agreement gave leadership roles in the transitional government to everybody who had a stake in the war. It was the only way they could stop the war, get Charles Taylor out and have peace in the country. The elections are just 18 months away. It was a peace agreement of convenience. And as for the senator... we had a few run-ins during the war. That's all.'

I knew it. Ben and Martin had been mercenaries. Probably still were, for all I knew.

'So, what's in the report?' I asked.

'It's the definitive report on the state of the diamond mines in Liberia. It also goes into detail about the people that run them and their other nefarious activities. The senator's included,' Grace answered.

She announced that the next stop was the UN headquarters.

'We're going to meet Mark Kroeker, the Police Commissioner, United Nations Mission in Liberia,' explained Martin.

'After that, we'll go to the Executive Mansion to meet with the National Security Adviser. If you're going to be nosing around asking questions on the mining industry and the bigshots that run it, then you need to know who you're facing. And if things go haywire, you need to know who you can run to. That's where the NSC and Mark come into the picture. Then, we'll head back to the hotel for meetings with Grace's people.'

The UN Mission in Liberia (UNMIL) headquarters was housed in the German embassy building. Mark Kroeker gave us his overview on the security situation in Liberia. All he could say was that Liberia was relatively stable although, as he said, 'the cooks that stir the stew of conflict are still very much in the picture.'

At the Executive Mansion, an empty tower block, we weren't told anything new by the National Security Adviser. Yes, the war was over. They had great hopes for the economy. The mines were a thorny issue, as they were still controlled by 'external forces'. If we wanted to conduct field studies at the mines, he couldn't guarantee our safety and, in any case, most of the equipment had been destroyed during the war.

Back at the hotel, I called Kemi. She sounded elated. *Didn't she miss me at all?* She filled me in about her return to work. Sharronne, the colleague she had a less-than-easy relationship with, had told everyone she wasn't coming back and that she, Sharonne, was going to bid for Kemi's job. However, Windy CEO was very keen for her to go to Leeds to start organising *World Star Baby*. The competition venue was a big issue. Windy CEO was adamant it had to be held in Leeds and wanted Kemi to go up there to look at some venues. And, finally, Yanis was fine. He was enjoying the nursery.

I tried not to feel like I wasn't needed; it was evident they were getting on fine without me. She held the phone to his mouth so I could hear his gurgles. At that moment, I wanted to be with them more than anything else in the world. I told her I loved and missed them both.

I didn't tell her about Grace. And I didn't tell her how bothered I was about the trip to Leeds she was planning. I resisted the temptation to cross-examine her about how long she would be away and what she was planning to do about Yanis. It would seem selfish. She was happy. Why spoil it? Maybe she would take Yanis T with her to Leeds?

'Any news from the estate agent about the house we were interested in?'

'I don't know. I haven't checked the messages.'

I couldn't help complaining a bit that she hadn't done this.

'Zack, I'm tired, your son is getting cranky, and I really do not want to argue with you. I've had a great day – tiring but still great. Yanis and I miss you. We said we would make this work and we will. We also said we wouldn't sweat the small stuff and you're freaking out on me already. You have to learn to let go. God's in control, not you.'

'I just miss you both, that's all.'

'What's it like out there? Are you okay?'

I didn't want to go there. Everything was so new and overwhelming to the senses: Africa, Liberia, the enormity of what Rhodenburg wanted to do here. I felt very negative about the bid. And *that woman*. Risen like a spectre from my past. But I didn't want to tell my wife these things. She had married a rock, not a spineless fool.

'This is going to sound really strange... but I would really like you to pray for me.'

Kemi went quiet. It was the first time I'd ever asked her to pray for me.

'Of course. Are you okay? I don't like the way you're sounding.'

'I'm fine. I'm just... I just don't know if being here is the right thing. There's so much to do and... '

'Zack?' She sounded worried. Yanis let out a small wail in the background.

'I'm just a bit tired, that's all.'

Yanis' wail was getting louder. I could sense Kemi's hesitation on the crackly line.

'Zack, is there something going on you don't want to tell me about?'

'Everything's okay. Go change our son's nappy,' I said.

'Zack, you're reading those daily Bible verses, aren't you?'

'Yes.'

'And the study Bible and the books Pastor Michael gave you?'

'Sure.'

I should've kept my mouth shut.

'No need to worry,' I assured her. 'It's all so... so new. War is evil. Do you think I'll make legal director?'

'I *know* you'll make legal director.'

As we were saying our goodbyes, Kemi said a Mr Jack Morris had called for me. She read out his number and I quickly wrote it down.

I had just enough time for another shower before going downstairs for the last appointment of the day – a meeting with some former mineworkers, set up by Grace. At 11pm Liberian time, I stumbled into bed and fell asleep as soon as my face hit the pillow.

14

I woke up early with Jack Morris and Grace battling for space in my mind. As was my newly acquired habit, I reached out for my daily Bible verses. It was Matthew 7:13 – *Enter through the narrow gate. For wide is the gate and broad is the road that leads to destruction, and many enter through it.* Not quite what I was looking for. I read on: *But small is the gate and narrow the road that leads to life, and only a few find it.* I ran my eyes to the bottom of the page where the study notes were. They talked about making decisions at great cost and living a life that was diametrically opposed to the world system. I put the devotional aside.

Whatever action I took towards that woman during this trip would be exactly what she deserved. She might have transformed herself into Nellie Mandela but I wasn't fooled. Deep down, she was still the same self-centred person she'd always been. And it was time she was exposed.

I needed to talk to Jack Morris. I sent Johnny to purchase more mobile top-ups for me and met with the rest of the team in the hotel restaurant at 7.15 for breakfast. At eight o'clock, we had our first visitor of the day: a former child soldier called George. Grace told us he was 13, though his wizened face and deepset eyes made him look decades older.

George told us he had no living family. Soldiers had come to his village, butchered all the men, raped the women and took some of them as their 'wives'. Both George's parents and his two siblings had been killed. Like the rest of the remaining village children, he was told that if he didn't go with the soldiers he would be killed too.

It was the soldiers or starvation. He'd been just eight years old. He did many things in the three or four years he was a child soldier that he wasn't proud of. Many times the soldiers injected drugs into his head and then for a time he stopped being scared to fight or do the other dreadful things they asked him to do. No, George didn't know why they were fighting. Many times he tried to run away but he didn't know where to run to. Besides, nobody wanted him. Everybody knew he was a child soldier so he always went back to the soldiers because they accepted him. George finished by telling us that he loved Aunty Grace because she gave him food and was teaching him to read.

'George was one of the child soldiers that came to Grace's house that night. He lives with her now,' Ben added, as he ushered the child from the room.

When he left, Maxine rolled her eyes and turned to Grace.

'All well and good – but I don't see what this has got to do with us. We're here to make an economic assessment of the mines and other potential sources of economic renewal, not to engage in social development programmes.'

Grace was quick to respond.

'This trip might be just business for you, but I want you to see that it's more than a set of economic theories; what you do will directly affect these people. When you go home and file your reports, I want you to see George's face and the faces of the mineworkers who came here yesterday.'

Maxine bit her lip. I knew her well enough to know that she wasn't interested in human interest stories. She liked cold, hard facts. That's why she worked in the City.

'Some feasibility trip this is turning out to be. If I wanted to save the world, I would've joined the Red Cross,' she muttered.

'Grace is a nurturer. She wants to adopt George,' Ben said.

Nurturer? I wanted to laugh out loud. A woman who'd had at least three abortions before she was 22? I felt her looking at me but refused to look her way.

I didn't feel very differently to Maxine. Grace's unorthodox way of handling this feasibility trip was rather unprofessional. We were meant to be having meetings with government ministers,

World Bank and IMF officials, maybe some development agencies. All we'd done was visit a senator that Ben and Martin had personal axes to grind with.

The meeting took a break and I excused myself and went up to my room. I tried calling John Morris. The call didn't go through. I left a message on Tristan's voicemail informing him of my attempts to contact Jack.

I sat down on my bed and looked at my Bible for a few moments. The day's devotional verse flitted through my mind. I hesitated. Being coldly honest with myself, I'd not really expected to find myself taking Christianity seriously. Saying the sinner's prayer had been an attempt to please Kemi, to oil the wheels of my life a little. Now, in Liberia of all places, I was uptight with God because nothing was going the way I wanted it to and I was angry.

I remembered a conversation months before with Michael's wife Janice, when I was denying God's existence.

Maybe he's always been there. The night your mother left you outside the orphanage, could he have led the woman that found you? Was there a plan for you being in the orphanage? Was it God who gave you your inner strength, so you would be strong for other people? Did he give you the ability to thrive and succeed in life against all odds? And the scholarship? And the ability to study law at university? Was it God who made a way for you to succeed in your career and other areas of your life? Zack, he's always been there.

I didn't answer her then and I doubt I could answer her now. I was agitated and restless. Sometimes I felt that all the parts of my life were coming together and sometimes I felt they were coming unglued. Like now.

I got off the bed and wandered to the window overlooking the street. I couldn't hide from it for ever. I had to do something about that woman... Grace. Her voice, her manner, her supposed love for this country and its people... nothing could erase what she'd done to me. I still hated her. And the more time I spent with her, the harder it was for me to control my dislike of her.

Oh, other people were taken in alright! And no wonder. In the eight years since we'd parted she had transformed herself into Mother Theresa. But I wasn't fooled. Beneath the dubious halo was the same woman who had killed my child.

And something else bugged me: her relationship with Ben and Martin, mercenaries turned security experts.

There was a knock on my door. Somehow I knew who it was. Sure enough, when I opened the door, there was Grace. I stepped aside and motioned for her to come in. As I did so, I saw Maxine heading along the corridor towards my room with determined steps. When she saw Grace, her steps faltered for a split second and then she took out a key and disappeared into her own room.

I closed the door. Grace's eyes swept the room, landing on my Bible. A bemused look creased her mouth. I wanted to smash it in.

'Some things don't change. You're still attracting them like flies to honey,' she said, jerking her head towards the door.

'Say what you want and leave.'

'It all happened eight years ago, Zachary. I've moved on and I think it's about time you did.'

'My name is Zack.'

'I'm trying to make this as easy for you as possible. I have no problems working with you. That's because the bigger picture is more important: the future of this country and its people. You have to decide for yourself what you can achieve by ruining your career – which is what will happen if you don't keep a rein on your feelings about me. I did what I thought was the right choice for me at that time. They tell me you're married now, and have a son. Why dwell on the past?'

'Perhaps you should leave before we both say things we would regret,' I said.

She nodded briefly but said no more. No sooner had she left the room than my mobile rang.

'You had me worried last night. Is everything okay?' Kemi asked.

'I'm fine. How's my son?'

'He's fine. Mum's coming in a few minutes. Dad says hello. He says not to forget your Foluke mission when you stop over in Lagos on your way back.'

'I wish you were here.'

'Zack, are you okay?'

'You worry too much. I've got to go. Have a meeting. I'll call you later,' I said.

15

We were going to one of the largest displacement camps in the country, about 10 miles outside Monrovia. Ben and Martin gave us a running commentary on the sights and sounds that we passed. We crossed Gabriel Tucker Bridge – the bridge that would for ever be remembered as the focus of heavy fighting during the war as rebel soldiers and government supporters fought to get control of the capital. I remembered the images beamed around the world of drug-crazed fighters wearing blonde wigs and make-up, throwing bombs and firing guns at will.

The bridge was also the gateway to Bushrod Island, near the port and warehousing owned by foreign merchants. Most of the warehouses had been destroyed during the war. There were lots of construction projects going on. We passed the market: a sprawling, bustling hive of human activity.

Grace took up the stream of information.

'There is only one cement-making company in Liberia – that's in a country of three million people. When doing your economic calculations, that's definitely something you should look at. Liberia is set to have the largest contingent of UN peaceworkers in the world. Yet, they have nowhere to house them! They can't build hotels and houses fast enough. There are hardly any roads; those that exist are filled with cavernous potholes. You've seen how empty the government buildings are; they were all pillaged during the war. Furniture, even roof tiles were taken; and what people couldn't take, they destroyed.'

'So, why exactly are we going to this displacement camp?'

Another question from Maxine, barely restraining her frustration. I felt the same way, but stayed silent.

'So you can see how a great percentage of Liberians live. After that, we have an appointment with the Minister for Lands, Mines and Energy. He has a lot to say on economic regeneration in Liberia,' Grace answered.

'I'm not sure we need the camp visit,' Maxine retorted.

'I'm trying to get you to think outside the box. Perhaps when we get to the camp, you will see why it's so important to have an economic programme based on social and economic transformation.'

'Purleeze!'

Maxine jutted her chin out and resolutely looked out of her window. The jeep continued its bumpy ride.

'Think of these camps as inner-city areas,' said Martin.

'People live and die in there. Children are born there. Businesses are conducted there. For many, life in a camp is all they know. They can't go back to their homes because they're not safe.'

Martin shook his head. 'I've been everywhere: Afghanistan, Bosnia, Iraq... but Liberia... '

'So why stay?' Maxine asked.

'Africa's like a drug. Once you visit, it's almost impossible to leave. Ask David Livingstone. And Grace!' Martin laughed at his own joke.

Finally, we pulled up outside a gate manned by a UN trooper who waved us in, winking at Grace. She waved back.

'We're not really allowed in the camps without authorisation but Dele, the guy that just waved, is a good friend of mine.'

Of course. Dele was also rather good-looking.

I was shocked at my own train of thought. I was doing a very good job of judging Grace. But wasn't my judgement right? I switched my attention to Ben.

'Condoms are the most precious commodity in these camps and Grace ensures that this camp gets a regular supply. She's being practical. The girls use sex for business. A lot of them are orphaned and heading households at very young ages. The churches do not like Grace much. They say she's encouraging teenage prostitution and sexual promiscuity. I guess she can't help but step on people's toes. Yesterday's senator is her number one fan. He's making plans to have her forcibly removed from Liberia. The only reason Grace is alive is because all those who wish her harm know she's under the protection of the UK and US governments. The Liberian people love her. I suppose in the end, that's all that matters.'

I noticed Grace smiling softly at Ben as he said that.

Our jeep made its way over the red earth road scarred with huge potholes. At the base of a steep hill, surrounded by heavy, thick forests, were thousands upon thousands of blue tarpaulin-covered huts.

Despite my longing to be back at the hotel or even back home in London, I had to see for myself if what I'd seen on television about these camps was true.

It was.

The camp held 20,000 people, with no electricity, no water and no sanitation system. Rivers of open sewage ran alongside groups of ragged children kicking a football. Their mothers squatted under the tent flaps, staring into the unseen distance. It was squalid and offensive. Bizarrely, we heard singing coming from a distance away.

Grace pursed her lips. 'That's all they ever do. Go to prayer meetings and sing. Drives me nuts.'

'You can say what you want, but I like it. If you lived in a pit like this, you would want to think there was some kind of divine exit plan.'

This, surprisingly, was from Maxine. She headed in the direction of the strains of *Amazing Grace* and we followed her.

We peered inside a hut. About 10 people sat on benches, another dozen or 15 stood. They all had their hands raised in the air, eyes closed, oblivious to us. No lead singers, no musicians. But the singing gave me goose bumps and I felt my heartbeat race a little. I looked around me. Were the others feeling the same? Ben and Martin stood politely; Maxine and Andy had bowed their heads a little. Grace was wearing her bemused face.

Did she have a heart at all? I wondered.

Slowly, by some strange group telepathy, the song died away. The singers opened their eyes and let their hands fall to their sides.

'We sing because even in the midst of suffering and incredible hardship, God is still God. We sing, not because we understand but because we give praise to him who does understand and in his infinite wisdom has chosen not to reveal some things to us. And we sing because when we sing we forget our present life. That is why we sing.'

The voice came from somewhere inside the hut out of our sight line. As if on cue, the group started singing again, this time in a local language.

Grace looked at her watch.

'We have an appointment with the medical programme officer. Those who want to do church can do that later. That's the problem with this continent. Religion!'

'Okay, okay. I think you should stop. This is not the time for your favourite rant.' Ben put his hand under her elbow and nudged her away from the hut.

'But it's true! So many fundamentalist agencies are coming into the camps and spreading their abstinence ideals. Who gave them the right to impose their views on other people? Who? And do you know what they're doing at their food distribution centres? I'll tell you! They're giving out Bibles to the food recipients and positively encouraging them to become *born again*. Even their anti-prostitution programmes have conditions. They tell the girls they *rescue* off the streets that they have to attend Bible studies otherwise they cannot participate in the programme.'

By this stage, her voice had risen. Ben told her to be quiet.

'I've had enough of them! I'm all for anyone practising their faith but what I absolutely object to is people using religion as a weapon to intimidate others into following their own agenda.'

'And whose agenda is that?' Maxine asked.

'Their fundamentalist religious agenda, that's what!'

'I don't see what the problem is. From what I've read in the briefing papers, it's often these so-called fundamentalist groups who are out there doing the aid and development work. They're asking girls they've taken off the streets to attend Bible classes. So? They're off the streets, aren't they? They're distributing Christian literature alongside their food aid packages. Big deal! At the end of the day, they don't have to read it. They're preaching abstinence. Well, if they're targeting teenagers who use their bodies to make money, why is that a problem? These fundamentalists are working in a country you say yourself the world has no interest in, much less cares about, and I think we should applaud them – not mouth off about *agendas*. I've been here just two days and I can't wait to get out. If anyone has a problem with the way these agencies are helping, then they should come here and try it themselves. Otherwise, we should let these people be.'

All this from Maxine. I was not the only one totally surprised at her words. Andy's mouth had difficulty shutting itself.

'Great speech. Now, can we go to the clinic tent, please?' Grace said brusquely, starting to walk away from us, with Ben still at her elbow.

'I got fed up with her superior attitude,' Maxine said in the silence that followed.

I couldn't help myself; I gave Maxine a big grin.

The clinic tent was staffed by about 20 volunteers, some of them nurses before the war. It was the only medical facility in the camp. The only doctor was not available as he was dealing with an emergency in another camp.

If Grace's intent was to overload us with the stench of human misery, she succeeded. Malnutrition, STIs, HIV, other diseases and conditions equally distressing – all were represented in the steady stream of patients. One queue was only women and girls.

'Rape cases. A particular malady of post-war countries,' Grace said, noticing me looking at the queue.

The reports I'd read in my City office had mentioned the pandemic levels of sexual and criminal violence that occur in post-war countries. But the reality was nonetheless distressing. Did Richard my boss have any idea about all this as he looked to the kind of economic regeneration that would benefit Rhodenburg? I doubted it.

I said a short prayer for my wife, son and – for the first time in my life – those who cared for me at the children's home. I thanked God that I wasn't born in a displacement camp, forced to live with the very people who destroyed my parents' home and livelihood.

Maxine and Grace were barely speaking to one another, and that was a little worrying. Maxine was a consummate professional. But, like Andy and me, she had come to Liberia expecting to visit diamond mines and talk to high-ranking financial experts. The only person of influence we'd seen was a former warlord, now transitional government senator. I hoped the meeting with the Minister for Mines would be more productive. This whole trip was beginning to look fruitless.

16

The Minister for Lands, Mines and Energy was arguably the most powerful man in Liberia.

Maxine, as the finance specialist on our team, had prepared well. She understood numbers. She could recite financial stats and make them sound like poetry. The meeting with the minister would set out the legalities of our bid and the details of the contract to be drawn up in the event we won.

Andy, as strategist, had the job of bringing together Maxine's and my conclusions and drawing up a combative strategy that would ensure we won the bid.

And me? Well, I was supposed to head up the team, be diplomatic, and concentrate on relationship-building for the future. I was keenly aware that I wasn't pulling my weight.

Our jeep stopped at the front entrance of a building with broken slats for windows.

'This used to be a government building, the Ministry of Social Affairs, I think,' said Ben.

'Like others we've seen, it was stripped bare during the war. Not a table left.' Martin hurried us inside.

Up a flight of stairs, we found ourselves in a dark corridor with locked doors on either side.

Our destination was a large room at the end of the corridor with an extremely efficient air-conditioner. Several people were seated, waiting expectantly, at a long table with documents on it. I felt an adrenaline surge, relishing the prospect of the cut and thrust of legal negotiation. Down to business at last!

Maxine began, 'Thank you very much, minister, for giving us some time in your very busy schedule. It's my first visit to Africa and it's been an absolute pleasure being here. I haven't seen such a lush country in my life!'

She flashed him her sexiest, most disarming smile. Thankfully, he smiled back.

We launched in, working as a team, extolling the virtues of Rhodenburg, boasting of its experience around the world. We handed the minister a report detailing our proposals and financial projections. I was trying to read him, with little success. The man was giving nothing away.

With an assurance that we would receive a response within 24 hours, the meeting was over.

Back in the hotel lobby, we discussed our expectations of the outcome. Andy had some concerns about the legality of any decisions reached.

'It's the legitimacy factor. International law is rather grey on this matter. Does a transitional government have the power to issue binding contracts for national resources, bearing in mind they are transitional?'

'Zack, what do you think?'

'The current government is a transitional one but it is a *legitimate* transitional government,' I offered.

'We have to bear in mind the competition factor. We have to get in here before anyone else does and conducting business with this *legitimate* transitional government is the best way to do it. I think it's a question of ensuring that everything we do is as open yet as contractually binding as possible so that, when the new government is voted in, they will have no choice but to carry on where the transitional government left off.'

Grace objected, 'I thought the whole point of this trip and this bid was to have something tangible and incorruptible for the *Liberians*. If all Rhodenburg is going to do is sign contracts with this transitional government that will ensure it has exclusive access to Liberia's mines, then it's not that different from the other mercenary outfits that have done precisely the same thing. The only difference is that Rhodenburg would not be trading guns in exchange for diamonds. You would be trading money and lives and *SWA* will not be a part of that. Does anybody remember East Timor?'

Maxine bristled. 'You bulldozed your way into the Rhodenburg bid and if you want to bulldoze your way out, that's fine.'

Martin held up his hands. 'Can we focus on the issue at hand? There's still a UN ban on exporting Liberian diamonds and, from what I hear, the ban will not be lifted anytime soon. At least, not before the elections take place.'

After more debate, we dispersed. I went upstairs to my room, wondering if I had bitten off more than I could chew. What Grace had said about Rhodenburg not being different from mercenary companies had hit home. Diamond mines had been fought over in other African countries. Thousands of civilians had been killed or displaced – hence the term 'blood diamonds'.

I hated to admit it, but I was questioning whether this was something Rhodenburg should be involved in. I wanted to be Rhodenburg Africa Legal Director – but at what cost? The mineworkers that came to the hotel two nights ago had told tales of woe and brutality at the mines they were forced to work in. George's face as he told his story also appeared before me. And the displacement camp; such misery and squalor I had never seen before and hoped never to see again.

And there was God. Whether or not I wanted to admit it, my reluctant Christian faith was beginning to matter to me. I knew enough of my faith to know that the direction in which the bid was heading was not entirely right.

On the other hand, this bid *would* help Liberians. If Rhodenburg didn't do it, somebody else would. The difference is that they would be trading arms, and bloodshed would inevitably follow. At least with Rhodenburg in partnership with *SWA*, there would be social development programmes that would profit all Liberians.

But did any foreign company have the exclusive right to Liberia's diamonds? I lay back on the bed. I thought of Kemi. And Pastor Michael.

I groaned and reached for my Bible, open on the bedside

table. My eyes fell on a verse: *The wicked plot against the righteous, and gnash their teeth at them; but the Lord laughs at the wicked for he knows their day is coming.* I flung it across the room.

I tried Jack Morris. This time, the call went through.

'Jack Morris? It's Zack... Zachary Kariba—'

'Hello?'

'Mr Morris? It's Zachary... '

'Hello, is anyone there?'

'Mr Morris—'

'Hello? Is anybody—'

I hung up and flung the phone in the same direction as my Bible.

* * *

After supper and an inconclusive team meeting looking at the options if the minister didn't like our proposals, Andy and Maxine headed for a beachside bar with Martin. Ben said he wanted an early night. Grace talked about going home.

I tried calling Jack again. No joy. But I did manage to speak to Kemi and Mark. I decided to spend the rest of the night getting to grips with the book of Romans. I liked the man's style; in fact, I thought the apostle Paul should've been a lawyer. There was certainly plenty to chew on.

For since the creation of the world God's invisible qualities – his eternal power and divine nature – have been clearly seen, being understood from what has been made, so that men are without excuse. For although they knew God, they neither glorified him as God nor gave thanks to him, but their thinking became futile and their foolish hearts were darkened (Romans 1:20,21).

His invisible qualities. I wondered what that meant. I read the study notes at the bottom of the page. It seemed that a lot of the things I'd always taken for granted were meant to be expressions of God's existence: the sun, the moon, the earth and all of creation. I read on, the fuzz starting to clear from my head. I flicked over the page, read a few verses and my heart stopped cold.

You, therefore, have no excuse, you who pass judgement on someone else, for at whatever point you judge the other, you are condemning yourself, because you who pass judgement do the same things (Romans 2:1).

Helen's face appeared before me. I shoved it away. It came back again. I read the verse again and put the Bible aside, thinking I wouldn't read any more. I would give up on Romans. But, almost of their own volition, my hands reached out for the Bible. I flicked through it again. And came upon another verse that stopped me dead.

This is then how we know that we belong to the truth, and how we set our hearts at rest in his presence whenever our hearts condemn us. For God is greater than our hearts, and he knows everything (1 John 3:19,20).

But, I wasn't passing *judgement* on anybody, was I? Grace exercised her legal right to kill ... I just had problems with the fact she murdered my own child. And I had serious issues with the way she was sabotaging Rhodenburg's work with constant interference and assertions of knowing what was best for Liberians just because she lived here. Her decision to exercise her full rights to sexual liberty by sleeping with whoever wasn't my business either. I just found it distasteful. That's all.

You are condemning yourself, because you who pass judgement do the same things.

Whoa! The voice was so clear, it was as if someone was right there in the room with me. *I* wasn't a murderer. *I* didn't abort babies. *I* was so much better than that woman. I debated with the voice.

Yet you're angling for sole rights to another country's diamond mines.

I'd had enough. I took purposeful steps towards the door. I needed diversion, company. Everyone was out except Ben. I was to going to hang out with Ben whether he liked it or not. I hesitated for a minute when I got to Ben's door and then knocked on it boldly. Grace opened it – wearing what was clearly Ben's shirt.

'I'm sorry,' I gabbled. 'I wanted to speak to Ben.'

She moved aside to let me in the room. I hesitated.

'I'll come back later.'

I turned to go. A hastily-clad Ben appeared by her side.

'Everything okay?' he asked.

'Sure... I just wanted to ask you something. I'll come back later.'

17

The next day, although Maxine came downstairs to breakfast looking as polished and sensual as ever, Andy looked rather the worse for wear. He poured himself an extra strong cup of coffee. Maxine leaned towards Andy and shouted 'Good morning!' in his ear. He blanched.

'Sorry. Couldn't resist,' Maxine said, smiling.

'Heavy night?' I asked, spreading butter on my toast.

'So-so,' she replied, not looking at me.

'Our Max here got herself a UN peacekeeper friend. Some Irish bloke. Where is he anyway? I thought he spent the night.' Andy looked round.

'At his checkpoint. Doing what he does best: keeping the peace. Now, what does a woman have to do to get some fried eggs and bacon around here?'

Andy looked like he was about to throw up.

* * *

There was a message at the hotel reception. The Minister for Lands, Mines and Energy had rung. He wanted to see us. I sighed in relief. A distraction at last. At his request, we went to meet him and one of his aides in the lobby of the Urban Hotel on Broad Street, in the city centre.

'I've had a look at your figures and spoken with my advisers. It looks good – but I do have a few questions.'

We all nodded. Not too eagerly though; we didn't want to appear desperate.

The aide leaned forward.

'There are others equally interested in the mines. Your proposal is by no means the only one that we're currently evaluating. We wondered why yours should be considered above the others.'

'Because our deal is for the good of Liberians and Liberia,' Andy replied.

The aide smiled faintly.

'We'll be in touch. Thank you very much.'

Was that all? I couldn't believe we had gone all that way for a 10-second meeting.

Back at our own hotel, Andy paced up and down.

'Ben, Martin... Do you know these competitors?'

'Some of them,' Ben answered.

'What are they offering that we don't have?'

'Well, what aren't they offering?'

Andy shot him a look and continued pacing.

We never did make it to the mines. The rest of the trip was taken up with several more cryptic meetings with the minister, who seemed to enjoy the games he was playing with us. I noticed Andy, in particular, getting more and more agitated as our departure day drew closer and closer. On our last day, he wasn't at breakfast. Ben said Andy had privately arranged a breakfast meeting with the minister's aide. I felt uneasy about that and Maxine didn't look too happy either.

* * *

When Grace came to the hotel to say goodbye, Ben pulled her aside and whispered something to her. I saw her look at Andy and purse her lips, but she said nothing.

'I sure will miss it though... in a way,' sighed Maxine, settling back in her seat as the plane took off later that day.

'It takes a trip like this to remind you how fortunate we are in London. Just imagine if war ever broke out in England. What would we do?'

* * *

Lagos was hot and humid, even at night. But I wasn't complaining. I was glad to be out of Liberia. I drank in the sights as we drove through to the hotel, wanting to capture everything so I could relay it to my wife verbatim. Lagos was pulsating. I daydreamed about bringing Yanis to his motherland. Yellow buses whizzed by, some with the conductors dangling precariously off the sides. All manner of religious declarations, Christian and Islamic, decorated them. Roadside billboards and posters promoted the latest church crusades, battling for people's attention alongside glossy adverts for mobiles and luxury cars.

'Are all Nigerians religious?' I asked our driver, Samson.

'Maybe, sir, it's just that life in Nigeria is so difficult that without divine intervention one would surely perish.'

'Is life so hard here? Somebody once told me that every Nigerian is a businessman,' said Andy.

Samson looked briefly at Andy in the mirror.

'That is very true. We are all struggling to survive. Whatever you get paid from your daily job is never enough because the cost of living increases every month. So people have no choice but to dabble in all kinds of business to get additional sources of income.'

At the hotel, Maxine and Andy happily expressed their intention to spend the evening at the bar. I murmured my apologies and waited in the lobby for Foluke. I had called her from the airport.

'We're going to the Londoner, a pub down the road. Is that okay?'

I nodded, enveloping her in a bone-crushing hug, at the same time remembering Femi's words of warning: 'Don't let Foluke take you on a wild goose chase around Lagos at night. We don't want you coming back as a corpse. The armed robbers on the streets there are getting more and more brazen by the day. And, whatever you do, don't wander out with your City slicker belongings on display.'

'It's been too long,' she said.

I was startled by how gaunt she was looking. The sparkle in her eyes had gone, replaced by a kind of inner weariness.

In a few minutes we were in the Londoner, a pub filled with European expats and affluent young professional Nigerians, mostly men.

'So, talk to me. What's all this about you and a penniless, gold-digger lover?'

Foluke waved her hand airily. 'Nothing much to tell. You tell me about Liberia.'

I told her briefly about the displacement camp, the people we had met and recounted some of the daily challenges faced by ordinary people.

'To think that all that is happening in the place you've just flown in from,' she shuddered.

'What about you? How are you doing?' I pressed her gently.

'I know that everyone thinks that I've messed up my life. But I've never been more sure of anything in my life. Lanre is not a gold-digger. It's not his fault that he was born without a silver spoon in his mouth.'

The waitress brought our two club sandwiches, a glass of Chardonnay for Foluke and a malt drink for me.

'After a couple of days in Liberia, I actually felt guilty when I ate because I knew that outside the hotel walls were people who didn't have access to the luxury of a proper meal.'

'Really?'

'Yeah. Lagos appears to be an alright city, though.' I played with the club sandwich.

'I love it. Life is stressful here but it's different. I don't feel as constrained as I used to in London. I'm a lot happier here. Can you believe my gallery is opening in a few weeks? Dad gave me the money for it. I think he thought that if he gave me the money, then I would let go of Lanre.'

'If you were married to Lanre, you would not be able to draw on your father's resources,' I reminded her gently.

'I know. But we're not married yet – so I might as well utilise the resources available to me!' She gave a dry laugh, then stopped when she saw my face.

'Zack, lighten up will you! Gees! I'm not like Kemi. Why do people always compare us? She was the one that got all the grades and walked straight into a good job after uni. She was the one that got the perfect man. Even the abortion drama has not diminished her in anybody's eyes because, in the end, she kept the baby and married the father. And, to top it all, she's gone religious and moral. I can't match that! I'm still trying to find my way and, yes, I'm 36 years old and not settled down yet. But please give me a break. I'm doing the best I can.'

'The family are worried about you.'

'I'm worried about myself, but the last thing I need is rehashed sermons on how I've messed up my life. I haven't. I love Lanre and I want to be with him.'

'Lanre doesn't have a job and from what Gail tells me he's sharing a room with three other men in Ajegunle, a notorious slum. Can you see why they think nothing adds up?'

'He's also a chemistry graduate.'

'Have you ever been to his place?'

'Yes. Once.'

'And?'

'And I haven't been back since because he doesn't like me going there.'

'Why do you think that is?'

'I thought you were on my side. Why are you doing this?'

I drew in a deep breath.

'Because, Foluke, you need to understand what you're letting yourself in for. If you marry Lanre, you can't go running to your father when things go wrong. It means saying goodbye to everything you've ever known, in particular your pretty affluent lifestyle. If you get married to Lanre and he's still living in a room with three other men in the slums, then that is where you will be. With him – as his wife. You've said you don't want to go back to the UK. What about him? What are his plans?'

'He... he wants to go to London,' she replied, glumly.

'And you're hoping he'll change his mind after you get married?'

She nodded.

'I just want to be happy. To have someone of my own,' she said brokenly. 'Why is it so hard?'

I reached out across the table and covered her hands with mine. Tears slid down her cheeks.

Our drive back to the hotel was quiet. As we said our good-byes, I hugged her and whispered in her ear. 'I know you've laughed at Kemi. But there's something in this Jesus stuff. Try it, Foluke.'

And I meant it. Perhaps for the first time. Maybe it was Liberia. Something had happened in my soul while I was out there, almost without my being aware of it. I gave her some photocopies of the pages from my daily Bible devotional I'd got done at the hotel.

'Not you as well!' She smiled at me through her tears.

'Yes. Me as well!' I hugged her again.

Back in my room, I sent my wife a text: *Can't wait to see you and Yanis. Counting the hours.* I knew she wouldn't reply as it was almost midnight in the UK. I ignored the plaintive knocking on my door and beamed a heartfelt thanks to God. I had a lot to be thankful for. I also tried saying a short, rambling prayer out loud for Foluke. I wanted her to be settled and happy in all she did. I felt silly praying like this. How could I be sure I was being heard? Still, I felt good.

18

The first thing I noticed was how cold London was. The second was that my wife had lost weight. Thirdly, that not many people were smiling. In West Africa, everybody smiled.

I spotted my family as soon as I emerged into the arrivals hall. Kemi pointedly ignored Maxine, but flashed a smile at Andy. Yanis was fussing in her arms. I took him and held him close to me for a few moments.

'Mrs Kariba, you look delectably wholesome,' I smiled, kissing her.

'And perhaps this young man wants a feed?'

'He's not the only one. Come on, the traffic will be murderous and I've got to get to work.'

'You're not serious.'

'I am. I've got a meeting in exactly two hours and the longer we stand here, the more likely I am to be late.'

She marched towards the car park. In the car, she tossed a baby bottle at me and asked me to feed Yanis.

'I thought we agreed to give him expressed milk?'

'Not any more. I don't have the time. The mornings are rushed enough as it is. By the time I get up, express, get him ready, get myself ready, get him to the nursery and get myself to work, I'm running on pure adrenaline. And in the evenings, I'm simply too tired.'

'So… you're weaning him… already.' It was a statement of my disappointment.

'Zack, it's 7am and I've been up since 3.30am because I wanted to pick you up from the airport. I've got to get you home, get myself to work and somehow convince a bunch of Americans that the greatest thing to happen on earth is *Singing Diapers* and *World Star Baby*. And I haven't had as much time as I need on my presentation because I've spent the whole week trying to convince people that just because I've taken maternity leave and now have a child, my brain hasn't turned to mush, that I can still do my job. Sharronne is still as sly as ever, waiting in the wings to take my job.'

'Okay. Let's not have this conversation while you're driving. I'm sorry. I didn't mean to stress you.'

She looked at me for a few seconds like she couldn't believe what she'd just heard. I knew she had been gearing up for an argument. Her tense shoulders eased a little.

'I'm really trying here, Zack. Just cut me some slack.'

Her favourite words.

'Of course.'

Yanis fussed the hour-long journey home. By the time we got off the motorway, his face was flushed and he felt very hot. We went straight to the hospital. Once again, the paediatrician reassured us there was nothing wrong. Babies got sick all the time. Like we didn't already know that! Kemi called the office and told them she couldn't make the meeting. Sharronne would go instead. After running all kinds of tests, the paediatrician concluded there was nothing wrong with Yanis. We made it back to the flat at noon.

Kemi's parents and Vanessa, having been alerted by mobile, were waiting for us outside. By this time, Yanis had fallen into exhausted sleep.

'It's okay. Just a fever. Nothing serious,' I said. I didn't want to see anybody. I just wanted to take my son inside and shut the door on the world.

Vanessa made cups of tea for everyone, while Kemi repeated what the paediatrician had said.

'Just a false alarm. Look at him now – sleeping like an angel!'

Gail stroked Yanis' moist forehead.

'Zack, you must be shattered,' she added, glancing at me.

I yawned. 'A couple of hours sleep ought to do it.'

Gail reached for her bag. 'I've brought you some food packages. Oh, and Foluke's father called. Whatever you did with Foluke worked, because she's broken it off with that boy.'

'Really? I didn't do anything, Gail. I just listened to her. That's all.'

My father-in-law stood up and drained his tea. 'Well, it worked. Come along now, Gail, Vanessa. Let's leave these two alone. The drama's over.'

When I woke, several hours later, Yanis was sleeping soundly in his cot. But Kemi had gone. I checked my mobile and there was a text: *Dashd into wrk. Bak soon. Luv xxx.*

I called Jack Morris.

'Jack speaking.'

'This is Zachary Kariba... from the home? Tristan said... I've been trying... '

'It's alright, son. I know all about it. Would you like to meet someplace?'

He sounded like just like the Jack I remembered. Kindly. I heard noises from the bedroom. Yanis was awake.

'I would like that very much, Mr Morris. There's a lot I need to know.'

'Tristan says you're a bigshot lawyer now. That true?'

'I'm a lawyer, yes.'

'Just like you always wanted.'

He remembered. Yanis' waking up noises were turning into a yell.

'Mr Morris, where can we meet?'

He gave me directions to a café somewhere in east London that would be easy enough to get to after work, and we arranged to meet the next day at 6.30pm.

I ran to the bathroom and emptied my insides into the toilet bowl. Despite my joy at being home and spending time with

Yanis, I had an anxious afternoon. Could I really go through with the meeting with Jack? Should I call Kemi to ask when she'd be home or would she think I was being a control freak?

It was past eight o'clock when a key turned in the lock and Kemi arrived, looking guilty. Had she forgotten she had a sick baby at home?

'I'm sorry,' she said. 'Sharronne's after my job and I'm not about to let her destroy everything I've worked so hard for.'

'And Yanis? What about Yanis?'

'He was with you. I knew he was safe.'

'It's not good enough.'

'Well, that's just too bad—'

'Have you even done anything about the—'

'Sort the wedding, go to work, take care of the baby, find a house... tell me, Zack, is there anything else you would like to add to your wife's "to do" list?'

I patted Yanis' back and made my way to the bedroom. She knew better than to follow me.

* * *

The next day, Andy, Maxine and I presented our findings to Richard. It was a long meeting. Richard was of the view that we should proceed with negotiating with the minister. Maxine voiced her concerns regarding SWA, while Andy maintained that we needed them. SWA gave Rhodenburg a heart, he repeated. As legal counsel, my job was to ensure that whatever decision they reached would stand up to scrutiny. But that first meeting came to an impasse. Richard called Helen and asked her to join us for a meeting the next day.

After work, my heart pounding despite all my efforts, I made my way to east London where I was meeting Jack.

Jack hadn't changed. He looked more fragile, yes, but essentially the same. I felt embarrassed that I hadn't kept up any communication with the home, but he didn't refer to it. He gave me a firm handshake.

'Zachary, my boy. I see things have turned out well for you.'

I shrugged, unsure. It was like I was eight years old all over again.

'And properly married as well. Good for you, son. Mind, you were never the sort to live with someone without marrying them first. Nothing wrong with those values. Nothing wrong at all.'

I shifted uneasily in my seat.

'Mr Morris—'

'You want to know what happened the night you were found outside the home?'

I leaned forward. 'Yes.'

The waitress came and asked for our order. Jack decided on omelette and chips. My stomach was churning. I asked for a glass of water.

'Seeing you today, in your suit an' all, does my heart proud. We saw all kinds come and go in that home, but I always felt you were something special. You had a way with you, Zack. Caused nobody no trouble from the day you were left outside that home to the day you moved on. You didn't give anyone cause to worry. But I must say I was a bit surprised... when you left for university you never called, never sent a postcard or nothing. You just left. Still... now, look at you.'

'I wanted to leave my past behind.'

'Hmm... but here you are now... unable to look to the future because you *need* the past you left behind.'

'I thought the home and everything about it would hold me back.'

'Lots of the kids made a clean break, but we never thought you would be one of them. Did you keep in contact with any of the kids?'

I shook my head, watching the bubbles float to the top of my glass.

'What were you running from?'

'Nothing. I just wanted to make something of myself. By myself.'

'I see. And, do you like being married?'

'Yes.'

'How long have you been married?'

Why all the questions? I just wanted him to tell me what I wanted to know and leave me alone.

'Not long. But we've known each other eight years.'

'Very good, son. Very good.'

I wished he would stop calling me 'son'. The waitress arrived with his omelette and chips and he tucked in. As I waited for him to finish I thought about Yanis. I hoped his mother hadn't forgotten him at the nursery. It would be just like her.

There I am, being judgemental again!

I was being unfair to Kemi. Sure, she wasn't perfect. But she wasn't the self-centred person I often made her out to be. It wasn't her fault that our careers happened to take on particularly crazy turns just when we were trying to adjust to being parents and being married. Perhaps I was the one at fault.

Jack pushed back his plate, reached into his back pocket and gave me a piece of paper.

'That's her, son. That's your mother.'

19

Many of the Samaritans from that town believed in him because of the woman's testimony, 'He told me everything I ever did' (John 4:39).

I don't know how I made it to Mark's house after leaving Jack at the café. But I found myself pressing his doorbell. Surprisingly, he was home. I knew he made visits to members of the congregation that frequently spilled over into the evenings.

He opened the door wide and gestured me in without a word.

'Vanessa is with Kemi, so you have all night,' he said.

I sat on the sofa and spread out the piece of paper on my knee.

'Here's my mother's name, telephone number and address. I've been trying to trace her for a few weeks. The current director of the home put me in touch with Jack Morris, the gardener at the home. He was there the night I was left outside the front door. I met up with him today and he gave me this.'

Mark glanced at the paper and back at me. He waited for me to talk but I didn't want to talk. I wanted answers.

'Does Kemi know about this?'

I shook my head. 'And I don't want her to know either. Things are a bit tense between us.'

Another silence while I tried to still my kangaroo emotions.

Then I went on.

'He had this information all these years and he never said a word. He said the right time never came. He wouldn't tell me anything more except that now I had all the information I needed and it was up to me what I did with it. I was so angry I walked out of the café. If I hadn't I would've assaulted him.'

'Zack, it's never a good idea to keep secrets from your wife. Especially something this big that affects the two of you. You should be dealing with it together.'

'My wife's head is filled with her job.'

'Give her a break! You're beginning to sound like a recording that's got stuck. You should think about supporting her, not about how everything affects you.'

'What should I do about this piece of paper, Mark? Now I have it in my hands, I don't know what to do with it. What do I do? Call her? Turn up on her doorstep? What?'

'I can't answer that, Zack. Only you can. But let me say this again: Kemi needs to know about this. All I can do is pray for you and with you.'

Prayer. I wanted someone to tell me what to *do* with the piece of paper that was burning a hole in my hands.

'Zack, now's the time for you to start taking hold of all that you've been taught over the last few months. You've read about it, argued for and against it at length... but unless you determine to live the Christian faith and apply its principles to your life, then it will be just something you're doing because it seems like a good idea. Nothing more.'

I didn't want to hear a sermon. Why wasn't he helping me?

'Look, as it happens... in Liberia, my faith became as real to me as you are.'

I stopped, wondering how much to say.

'I ran into that woman in Liberia... the woman I was with before Kemi. Remember? She aborted our child. Of all things, she was assigned to our team by an organisation we were working with.'

I laughed mirthlessly.

'I thought God was having a joke at my expense. But things started happening to me.'

I told him about the voice I heard accusing me of judging Grace and my desire – insatiable at times – to read the Bible.

Mark put his hand on my shoulder.

'It's the Holy Spirit at work, stirring up your heart and awakening your inner person to his presence and your conscience. You needed to run into Grace so you could forgive her and move on. Probably, even now, she had too much of a hold over you. Maybe that's why you exert so much pressure on Kemi.'

He didn't understand and I felt angry.

'I don't need to forgive anybody anything! That woman has no hold or impact on my life. I have a wife and a beautiful son. And now, a long-lost mother. Do I sound like someone who needs to move on? And as for me putting pressure on Kemi... That's ridiculous!' I laughed again.

'I don't know what you should do, Zack. Why not ask God?'

'Yes, well, thanks for everything.'

I grabbed my jacket and went home. Kemi and Vanessa were sitting at the dining table when I walked in. Kemi rose hesitantly when she saw me, trying to gauge my mood.

'We were just working out some stuff about the bridesmaids' dresses. I've spoken to Brent Hall and it *is* available. I was going to book it... but I wanted to check with you first.' She sounded nervous.

'Zack, are you okay? I just put Yanis in his cot.'

'I'm fine,' I replied, heading for the bedroom. Except my voice shook. The piece of paper was still burning a hole in my pocket.

'Can you have a look at the caterer's estimate for me when you have the time?'

'Sure.'

'Are you sure you're okay?'

'I said I was fine,' I said sharply.

I shut the bedroom door behind me. Then I took out the piece of paper, took my mobile out of my jacket pocket and dialled the number. It took three attempts because my hands were shaking so much. My heart felt as if it would jump out of my chest. Eventually, I dialled the right number and it rang. I'd made sure I dialled 141 to hide my mobile number just in case whoever picked up decided to call me back.

'Hello?'

It was a woman's voice. I hung up and I spent a few minutes looking at Yanis in his cot. Should I call again? I had to talk to my mother and find out why she had abandoned me. I had to see her.

* * *

I wasn't a big fan of conference calls but they served their purpose. Helen hadn't been able to come to the office but was on the phone and it was turning into a protracted meeting. We were going over the same ground again and again.

'Grace has very legitimate concerns about Rhodenburg's Liberia strategy and until those concerns are addressed then I'm afraid *SWA* will have to withdraw its support and partnership for this bid.'

Richard rapped his fingers on the table.

'I've told you already: she has no grounds for concern. Andy's proposals make us winners on all fronts – legal and moral – so what is the problem?'

'The problem is your lack of guarantees about what will happen after certification is granted, should Rhodenburg be granted exclusive diamond mining rights. We need to be sure your approach is different from the mercenaries'.'

Richard signalled for Maxine to take that one.

Maxine kept her voice neutral.

'Well, for starters, we will have invested millions of pounds in mining infrastructure and raised Liberia's diamond mining industry to international standards. *Nobody* has ever done that. Secondly, we would be training *Liberians* with a view to having a *Liberian* majority workforce in management positions. Again, no one has ever done that. Most of the renegades who have been offered mining rights simply employ locals to sift for diamonds. Nothing more, nothing less. Thirdly, *SWA* stands to gain from this because the programme would specifically target ex-rebel soldiers and give them sustainable and long-term employment, thereby keeping them out of temptation's way. Added to these proposals are the plans for free adult literacy classes from *SWA*. The classes would be on a much larger scale than you're currently doing and would be entirely financed by Rhodenburg. So, everybody wins. Explain to me once again why you have moral objections to this.'

Helen took a deep breath.

'Grace mentioned a decision to have binding contracts with the transitional government that would guarantee Rhodenburg access to the mines after the democratic elections next October. And what we also heard is something about offering the minister a little something to help him make his mind up?'

I looked at Andy. He shifted in his seat.

'Grace misunderstood,' he offered. 'I... we made no such suggestions. My team will confirm that.'

Richard took the initiative again.

'Helen, tell you what. Let's say we leave this today? The team will be going back to Liberia in a fortnight. I think everything will be much clearer after another visit. Let's hold off until then.'

'Richard, I'm not trying to make your lives difficult,' replied Helen. 'I just want you to look at this from *SWA*'s point of view. Imagine a company demanding exclusive rights to England's apples. Sounds ridiculous but this is what in effect you're proposing to do in Liberia with its diamonds.'

'Helen, we *are* an investment bank. We're in the business of making money and access to those mines is the best way of clawing back the costs of getting the mines up to par.'

'You're right. We should reconvene at another time. Have a good day.'

Richard pressed a button on the phone and turned to Andy.

'What *little something* for the minister?'

'She misunderstood. Honest, she did.'

'Yes, that's what I thought. Alright everybody, meeting over.'

Back at my desk few moments later, I received an email from

Maxine: *Andy's lying.* I deleted it immediately from both my inbox and trash.

20

It was a smart house in an up-and-coming fashionable part of London. I stood in the street for a while just hoping that a woman would step out of the front door. Nothing happened. I knew that if I stood around for too long my behaviour would look suspicious. What was stopping me from ringing the bell and announcing, 'Hello. My name is Zack Kariba. I'm looking for Miriam Abdul Rasaak. I believe she's my mother.'

I detoured to Gail and Femi's house to pick up my son. He now spent one day every week with them. When he saw me, his face lit up. He gurgled and put his chubby legs up in the air.

'You alright, Zack?'

I busied myself strapping Yanis in his carseat.

'Good. Work's been crazy but... ' I shrugged.

'And how's your church malarkey going?'

'Very well. I guess we should be going. Thanks for everything, Gail. Say 'bye to granny.'

Gail kissed my son's head. He smiled and a huge drool of saliva dripped down his chin.

'Look at his swollen gums and rosy cheeks. He's going to start teething soon.'

Kemi wasn't home when we got in. I didn't want her working late again. I wanted her with me so that I could tell her about Liberia, about Grace, about what was going on at work, about Jack Morris. And about my mother. I wanted her to stroke my forehead and cook my favourite meal instead of the takeaway that was going to be my dinner. I wanted things to go back to the way they used to be before *stuff* started happening.

I placed my son on his blanket in the middle of the room and pottered around the kitchen. I was delaying the inevitable. I knew what I was going to do.

Finally, I called the number again – but hung up again when I heard a woman's voice.

Fool! Why did you hang up?! To think your wife thinks you're some kind of rock. Ha! Ha!

Kemi didn't get home until ten o'clock, by which time I was mad at her for not being around when I needed her. She got ready for bed, watching Yanis in his cot, then lifting him out and smothering him with kisses. I pretended I was asleep.

The next morning, she told me she had go to Leeds for a couple of days.

'And Yanis. What about him?'

'The show's in five months and we haven't got a venue. I got word from James that the Americans were rather too pleased about Sharronne's presentation and were thinking of using her as the consultant for the US version of *Star Baby*. Apparently, she let it drop that I'd just come back from maternity leave and, with a baby to take care of, I wouldn't be as available as *she* would be. Any which way I turn, it seems my career is a disaster waiting to happen.

'Look, you wanted me to sort out the hall and I did. I'm still waiting for you to give me the go-ahead so we can secure it for December 15th. You wanted to know about the wedding plans. I left you the figures to look at and you haven't said a word. And you're being moody and secretive. You think I didn't notice that you went into the bathroom this morning to make a call on your mobile?'

'I just asked you who would take care of our son while you were gallivanting in Leeds.'

'Gallivanting. That's what you think I'm doing. *Gallivanting!*'

'I'm just asking you to put his needs first. That's all.'

'Zack, did you really think I would go to Leeds for two days and leave my baby son behind in London? Is that what you think about me?'

'It's hard to see that he matters that much to you.'

Kemi paled and tears came to her eyes.

'What has come over you? Ever since you came back from Liberia, all you've done is criticise and snap at me. I ask you about the trip, you won't talk. I ask you about work, you tell me not to worry. I tell you that Pastor Michael called to say hello to you, you tell me you want to be left alone. There's something eating at you but you won't tell me what it is.'

I turned away. I hated seeing her cry. I knew she was right.

'I have a lot of things on my mind. That's all,' I said. 'Let's not make a big deal about this. I've got to get to work. I'll drop Yanis at the nursery.'

Kemi wiped her nose with the back of her hand and looked at me with reddened eyes.

'Fine,' she said.

* * *

What to do about Andy was an issue that had to be tackled but I didn't want to say anything unless I had evidence that he did indeed have plans to bribe the Liberian minister. Rhodenburg had a strict anti-bribery policy. Andy was aware of that. He wasn't the kind to throw caution to the wind. On the other hand, if what Maxine said was true, it was only a matter of time before word got out about it. If it surfaced that I had knowledge of it and had done nothing...

I had to find out the truth, which was impossible without talking to Maxine. Discretion was paramount, so I couldn't talk to her during office hours. Meeting up with her after work was not an experience I particularly relished. I always made sure we were never alone. I didn't want my private life being the source of office gossip.

At the office that morning I tried without success to block my wife's reddened eyes from my mind. My mobile rang. It was Jack Morris.

'Have you spoken to her?'

'No.'

'I'm sorry, Zack. I've thought better of it... I wish I'd handled things better. Can you meet me at the café again, after work?'

'What's with the secrets?'

'Perhaps when we meet... '

'Fine. Tomorrow, after work. Is that alright with you?'

Michael called me around lunchtime. He wanted to know if I could make our regular meeting that evening. I said no. I was picking up my son from the nursery.

'Not a problem. We'll meet at your place. Mark and I will be at yours at about seven o'clock. That okay?'

It wasn't okay but it would've been rude to refuse.

I sent Kemi an email letting her know we were expecting visitors that night. She sent me an icy reply: *No problem.* Maxine spent the whole day looking in my direction but I ignored her. If she had information that Andy was offering bribes to the minister, why didn't *she* confront him about it or, better still, go to Richard herself?

I left work early and went to pick up Yanis. The nursery assistant mentioned that he was teething. It was almost July and summer had finally come to London. I took Yanis to the park and tolerated the understanding smiles of the mothers when we went past them. I sat on a bench with Yanis in the buggy in front of me. Hard to believe he was teething. He should be at home during the day with at least one parent with him, not a nursery assistant.

I wasn't going to think about Jack Morris, work, my wife or my mother. I was just going to sit in the park and enjoy being with my teething son. But Yanis wasn't having any of that. His face puckered, turned red and he opened his mouth wide. I let him cry for a few minutes then changed his nappy. But even a clean nappy didn't solve his problems. I drove home, stopping off at a pharmacist for some teething gel.

After giving him his bottle, I'd barely settled Yanis in his cot and switched on the baby monitor on the coffee table when the doorbell rang. It was Mark and Michael, armed with Bibles and smiles. I squashed the feeling of irritation that came over me when I saw them.

'It's been quite a job getting hold of you since you got back,' Michael observed, making himself comfortable on the sofa.

'You know how it is with work and everything,' I replied.

'So, what was Liberia like?'

'Enough to put you off war for ever.'

I found myself telling them about the displacement camp, the bullet-ridden buildings, the lack of running water, electricity and survival basics. And the churches. I told him about the churches everywhere and the little fellowship meeting in the camp.

'And you, how've you been?'

'You know... a lot on at the office, Yanis, moving and this wedding... every day is just another long list of things to do.'

Mark obviously hadn't told him anything about my mother, like I knew he wouldn't.

The meeting did not go too well. I knew I was resisting all their best efforts for me to open up. When they heard Kemi turn the key in the lock, they stood up and said their goodbyes.

Kemi went straight to the bedroom to check on Yanis before changing out of her office clothes.

'I really hate it when we fight or aren't talking to each other.'

'I'm sorry,' I said.

'Not good enough,' she replied. I got it. She wanted me to beg.

'You're not being fair,' I said.

'Good. Then you know what it feels like.'

She took a readymeal from the fridge and flung it into the microwave. Slamming the door, she punched some buttons in quick succession.

'Kemi, come on. You know how much I hate it when we argue, too. I've just got a lot of stuff on my mind and I'm trying to make sense of it all.'

'What stuff?'

'I can't really talk about it right now because I'm trying to figure it out in my head. I said I was sorry.'

'For what? What are you sorry for? Just words. Why can't you talk to me about this stuff that's going through your head? If you can't talk to me, then who are you supposed to talk to?'

The microwave pinged.

'I'm sorry for saying all those things about you and Yanis.'

Her hands paused halfway to the microwave door.

'You hurt me, Zack. What's happening to us? I thought we were going somewhere. You were reading the Bible and really getting into it. We were doing church stuff together. I know something happened to you while you were out in Liberia even if you refuse to discuss it with me. I've seen the way you read the Bible now. It's different. Like what you're reading is really going in there,' she said, pointing to my heart. 'So talk to me about it.'

I stood in front of her and put my hands on her arms.

'I will Kemi. But will you let me deal with it and sort it out in my head first?'

'I just want to help. You don't want to marry me in church any more. Is that it?'

'Don't be silly.'

'Is it that Maxine woman? I saw the way she was looking at you at the airport.'

'How can I look at Maxine when I know what you will do to me if I ever dare think of doing such a thing?' I smiled at her. She smiled back.

I kissed her forehead and we both stood in the kitchen for a few moments, just holding each other.

Later, in bed, I told her about hearing the voice in my hotel room in Liberia. I also told her about reading the Bible and the way it was making me look at myself. But I didn't tell her about Grace. I didn't feel ready. We talked for a while about everything and nothing, the way we used to before Yanis was born, when we had all the time in the world. It felt good.

21

Around lunchtime the following day, I had a call from Mark. He was in the area and did I have time for a quick lunch? I scanned my diary and said yes.

Over cappuccinos and salad bowls in Starbucks, I told him about Rhodenburg's plans for Liberia, about Andy's alleged bribe offer to the Liberia minister and about Maxine's message. He listened quietly until I'd finished.

'Well Zack, what you're going to do?'

'I don't know. I'm still trying to figure it out in my head.'

* * *

I made sure I got to the café about 15 minutes before the scheduled time and meditated on the day's Bible verse: *The mind of sinful man is death, but the mind controlled by the Spirit is life and peace* (Romans 8:6). I asked God to give me the peace of the Spirit.

As it turned out, Jack had plenty to say – answers to some of the questions that had plagued me all my life. He'd known all along.

'You're half Eritrean and half Italian. Your mother is now a married woman with three children: two girls and one boy. Her husband is some Eritrean businessman. They live in exile here in London at the address I gave you. She was an Eritrean student in London in the 1970s and very much in love with her Italian boyfriend. Her parents were very influential people.

She found out she was pregnant and asked me to help.'

I felt stunned. At least now I knew my race.

'You mean, you were involved, the night I was left outside the home?'

'Yes.'

'Why didn't you stop her?'

'Listen. This is the way it was. She was in her final year when she fell pregnant. She couldn't go back to Eritrea with a baby in tow. And not just any baby. A mixed-race child. Her parents had firm views about educating women, but getting pregnant outside marriage and to a foreigner was something else. The boy – your father – also made it clear that he wasn't interested in being a father. I don't think abortion ever crossed her mind. But she couldn't go back home to Eritrea with a mixed-race baby. It just wasn't done in Eritrean society.'

He stopped. I urged him to continue.

'You mustn't judge your mother.'

'How did you know her?'

'Her parents had a house in Hampstead and they wanted to be sure that their daughter would be safe so they hired my wife Maureen and myself to look after her. She was the only member of her family that was in England, you see. I was the gardener and jack of all trades while Maureen cooked and kept house.

'We warned her about the Italian boy but she wouldn't listen. Oh, she was crazy about him! Absolutely crazy. Everyone knew it would end in tears. Like I said, she found out she was pregnant in her last year of uni. With her going back to Eritrea, the house was put on the market. Maureen and I were looking for other jobs and that was when the opportunity came up for us to work at the home. They were looking for a cook and a caretaker-cum-gardener.

'Well, it was getting closer and closer to the time for the baby to arrive and for her to go back home and still she didn't know what to do about you. We were still trying to keep an eye on her. But then, one weekend, Maureen and I went to Wales. She has family there, you see. The night we came back, there you were, on television. A mite of a newborn with the police making appeals for your mother to come forward.

'She knew what she was doing. She knew that by dropping you outside the home, with Maureen and me working there, we'd make sure you were okay. A week after, we got a letter from her from Eritrea. There was only one line: *Take care of him.*

'Over the years, she kept us informed now and again of what was happening in her life. She sent us a pictures of her wedding. The man was the Eritrean ambassador to England. Maureen passed away when you were about eight. Cancer. I wasn't so good at keeping in touch after that. Sometime during the 1980s, your mother and her husband fled to London and have been living in exile since. There you have it.'

'I need to see her,' I said, half talking to myself.

'It's up to you, son. She'll be proud of you. I'm proud of you. You've turned out real well.'

We both stood.

'I'm very sorry, Mr Morris. It was a terrible thing I did, not keeping in touch when I left the home.'

'I won't say it didn't hurt. But you were trying to find your way.'

I had one more request.

'Mr Morris... '

'Yes, son?'

'Would you mind very much if I... called you once in a while? It's just that—'

'I would like that very much, son. I would like that very much.'

In less than an hour I was again standing outside my mother's house, hoping she would come out and praying that she wouldn't. After a few minutes I went home.

* * *

Kemi had decided to take Yanis with her to Leeds. The next morning was a flurry of activity as she got everything together. Kemi kept looking at me, as if she wanted to say something but was trying very hard not to.

When the cab honked outside, she hugged me very tightly.

'We'll miss you very much,' she said.

'Not as much as I'll miss you both. You sure about taking him with you?'

'Yeah. The office is providing a nanny service. Only because Windy CEO still insists on dealing with no one but me on this. The train tickets are first class. Did I tell you that?'

She hugged me tight again. I put the bags in the cab and waved them off. At the office I felt like I was just going through the motions. At 5.30pm on the dot I switched off my computer, and left for my mother's house. When I got to the front door, I didn't hesitate. I pressed the doorbell long and hard. The door opened and there she was. My mother.

We both stood for the longest time, looking at each other. She was small and very beautiful, with the deepest dark eyes. She didn't need to ask who I was, because she knew immediately. I had the sense of looking sideways into a mirror.

'Who's there, Miriam?' a voice called from inside the house.

A look of panic crossed her face. She started closing the door. When I reached out my hand to stop her, she looked straight at me.

'Don't ever come here again,' she said, and shut the door in my face.

What had I been expecting? A tearful and repentant reunion? I should have known that would've been too easy.

There it was. I wanted to see my mother. And I had. I wanted to know what she looked like. Now I knew. I wanted to know why she left me outside the children's home. Jack had explained it to me. What more did I want or expect?

I lifted up my hand to ring the doorbell again and saw the front room curtain twitch. She was watching me. My hand fell limply to my side. I couldn't do it. She gave birth to me but that did not give me automatic rights to destroy the life she had made. She didn't owe me anything.

And yet... In that house were three people who shared the same mother as me. They saw her every day of their lives. She had wiped their noses when they were babies, much like I wiped Yanis' nose. She had gone through sleepless nights as they teethed, ran fevers or developed rashes. But not for me.

Did she ever think about me or my father? Did she sometimes

look at her children – my siblings – like I looked at Yanis? Did she wonder what I was doing? Or ask herself if things would have been different had she taken me back to Eritrea with her?

I turned away and staggered out into the street like a drunk. The pain I felt was physical. And deep. My mother had denied me, her own son. What was so evil, so terrible about me that the women with whom I had significant relationships felt they had no choice but to hurt me?

My mobile bleeped. Maxine's name flashed on the glowing blue screen. I let it ring and wandered to a bus stop where I sat on the bench. I needed to think. I needed to lick my wounds. I needed to be alone. My mobile rang again. When it didn't stop ringing, I picked it up.

'Yes?' My voice was a dull monotone.

'Hi, why didn't you answer? We need to do something about Andy.'

'Not now, Maxine. I'm a bit busy,' I intoned.

'Zack, he's up to no good and we need to stop him. Andy wants this bid to propel him into the big league and he's willing to do anything to get there. If that means offering the minister's aide a bribe, then he will. I know he's working towards it, that's if he hasn't done it already. Imagine what will happen if the minister turns round and announces to the world that Rhodenburg's so desperate to get its hands on Liberia's diamonds, they offered his aide a bribe. It will be a catastrophe and you need to stop it.'

'Why do *I* have to stop it?'

'Because it affects us all. Andy really wants to make a splash because he hasn't done anything since China. He thinks Liberia's so tucked away in Africa, nobody would notice... '

'Maxine, can we talk about this another time. My hands are rather full at the minute.'

'Zack, he's convinced Richard that you and I do not need to go to Liberia with him on the next trip. I overheard him talking to Richard in his office. He said that you had already provided the legal framework for the bid and subsequent contract in the event we won and that, as my figures were constantly evolving, there was no need for me to come with him either.

Can't you see what's going on here?'

I could. I just didn't care.

'Zack? Are you there?'

'I'll see you on Monday, Maxine. Bye.' I hung up. It rang again straight away. *Shining star* flashed on the screen. Kemi.

'I just wanted to check you were okay. Yanis is settled in. He spent two and a half hours on the train screaming his head off. I've never been so embarrassed or suicidal in my life! I don't know why I thought bringing him to Leeds was a good idea. The nanny seems okay, though. So far, anyway. We'll see how it goes. How are you doing down there? I hate thinking of you all alone in that flat.'

'I'm alright.'

'You don't sound it.'

'Just hurry up and come back.'

'The weekend will go sooner than you realise. I can hear traffic. Where are you?'

'At the bus stop. Debating whether or not to go to Mark's,' I lied.

'Spoke to Vanessa on our way here. Give them my regards.'

'Yes. The bus is here. Gotta go. Big kiss to Yanis.'

'Bye and don't forget to drop off the deposits for the hall and the caterer.'

'Okay. Bye.'

22

My own mother didn't want to know me. Why?

The question reverberated around my head. Perhaps Jack had known what she would do. That was why he'd been reluctant to tell me things. If I had listened more closely to his words, I would have heard what he had been trying to tell me all along: *You mustn't judge your mother.* And my father? Where was he? In Italy somewhere with his own family perhaps, his dalliance long forgotten. It wasn't right.

What now, God? What am I supposed to do?

The Spirit helps us in our weakness. We do not know what we ought to pray for, but the Spirit himself intercedes for us with groans that words cannot express.

The weekend passed in a blur. I thought about going back to my mother's and making a nuisance of myself at her front door. I thought about calling Andy to talk about Liberia. On Sunday I went to church, but nothing much registered. In the evening, I ironed some shirts and looked at my work diary ready for the week ahead. On Monday morning I read my Bible devotional on my way to work: *He who was seated on the throne said, 'I am making everything new!' Then he said, 'Write this down for these words are trustworthy and true'* (Revelation 21:5). I wanted to believe those words.

At work, Richard announced that Andy would be going to Liberia on his own. Maxine didn't protest. I battled with keeping my mind on work. And lost. At lunchtime, I packed my briefcase and headed home, ignoring the looks from the rest of the staff. Not that I cared. One of the few perks of being Senior Adviser was the privilege of dictating my work hours. I rarely used the privilege but today...

I walked past my mother's house, hoping to catch sight of my siblings. Nothing. I so badly wanted to walk up to the front door again and press the doorbell but resisted. She had made it clear that she didn't want me. I was 30 years old. Why was that so difficult for me to understand? I had a wife and child, a great job, supportive in-laws, good friends. And now, it seemed, a relationship with God himself. I should be grateful. Not moaning about what I didn't have.

So, what if my mother left me at a children's home? At least, she cared enough to carry me to full term. So, what if she wasn't interested in having a motherly relationship with me? Gail had done more than her fair share in that respect. It was time I got rid of my ridiculous fantasy of a tear-filled reunion with my mother and got on with the daily business of living. I'd done alright without my mother all my life. I didn't need her.

Besides, I now had Jack Morris. If I wanted any links with my past, I would find them in that home and in the form of the kindly Jack Morris and all the other people that took care of me. I should be chasing after them, not some Eritrean woman who gave birth to me but had absolutely no interest in my life.

It was time I started living in the present instead of looking to my past and allowing it to hold me hostage. But, despite all my reasoning, my mother's rejection still hurt.

* * *

Back at the flat, I pottered about waiting for Kemi and Yanis. Finally, I heard their cab pull up outside the flat.

Kemi was exhausted. She passed Yanis to me and flopped onto the sofa.

'Haven't slept all weekend. I will not be doing *that* again with a baby. What was I thinking? Windy CEO was great with Yanis though. Loved him. Absolutely loved him. But I will not be doing that again,' she said, yawning.

'You're rather quiet,' she went on, registering my silence.

'You've paid the deposit for the hall and caterer?'

I shook my head.

'What were you doing all weekend? I ask you to do two tiny things for us, Zack, and you can't even do them. If that was you asking me, I wouldn't hear the end of it. That's just great! Wonderful! Something else for me to do. At least, tell me the papers for the new house have come through the post. The sooner we put pressure on that solicitor the better.'

I laid Yanis on his blanket and took her hand in mine.

'What's happened?' Her tone changed from nagging to fearful.

'I found my mother.'

Kemi breathed a sigh of relief.

'Don't be ridiculous. How can you find her when you don't even know who she is?'

'I do. She's Eritrean and my father's Italian. And there's something else I need to tell you. When I was in Liberia, I ran into that woman... Grace. She was our liaison person the whole time we were there.'

'That woman... '

'Yes.'

Kemi was finding the information overload a bit much. I shouldn't have thrown all this stuff at her the minute she came back from Leeds exhausted. It was a selfish thing to do. But then, had I given much thought to my wife in the last couple of months?

I told her everything: the email to the home, meeting Tristan, Jack Morris and finally going to see Miriam, my mother.

'You did all this without telling me.' Her voice was flat.

'I know. I'm sorry. I didn't want to bother you.'

'I can't believe you spent a whole week in Liberia with Grace without telling me. Isn't that what marriage is about?! How could you do this to me?'

'Quiet! You'll wake Yanis,' I cautioned her.

'I'll shout if I want to and there's nothing you can do to stop me!'

'I'm so sorry.'

'You've said those words more in the short months we've

133

been married than in the eight years we've known each other.'

It was true.

'So. What now? What am I supposed to do with all this information, Zack? What?'

'I don't know.'

'Well, neither do I.'

'What about work? If you're going to be working with Grace, then we need to do something.'

'I'm not having anything to do with that woman.'

'You need to... to forgive her and let us move on with our lives.'

'I don't need to forgive anyone anything and she doesn't have any hold over our lives.' Now it was me that was shouting.

'That's what you think, but I know better. You're full of hatred for her and you have been ever since I've known you. It's almost as if she's been there between us sometimes. And your mother. She's another ghost in your life, haunting you. Unless we deal with the two of them, we will not be able to move forward.'

'I'm not listening to this... this psychobabble!'

'Suit yourself.' Kemi brushed past me and went into the kitchen. But she came back a few minutes later with two mugs of hot chocolate.

'What are we going to do about your mother?'

'Nothing. She doesn't want to know.'

'And this Jack Morris. Can Yanis and I at least meet him?'

'We'll see.'

I concluded the conversation by turning on the television news. Only I couldn't concentrate. I knew Kemi was right. I had to let go of that woman and my mother.

Later that evening, Mark and Vanessa came round and we actually had a pleasant time together. We talked with them about that woman and my mother. Mark did not let on that he knew about them before Kemi had, for which I was grateful.

'Thanks for sharing all this with us. Actually, there's something we need to tell you two,' Vanessa said.

I saw her reach for Mark's hand and clench it tight. Kemi and I looked at the two of them expectantly.

'It's okay, I'll say it,' Mark said. He took a deep breath.

'I'm infertile. I got the test result this morning,' he said.

'We still haven't told both our parents,' added Vanessa. 'Don't know how to, really. Mark's the oldest and there are expectations... '

Vanessa's voice broke. Kemi and I looked at each other. Whatever our challenges with Yanis, I doubt we could imagine our lives without him now.

'I'm sorry,' Vanessa sniffed.

'Don't be silly,' Kemi said.

We heard snuffles on the baby monitor.

'Can I see little Yanis?' Vanessa asked.

'Of course. Come on,' Kemi said. They disappeared together into the bedroom. There was an awkward silence between Mark and me.

'Anything else I should know about your mother?' Mark asked.

'I've told Kemi everything. You were right; I should have done that earlier. She says that until I forgive that woman and my mother, I won't be able to move on with my life.'

'I think she's right.'

'Hogwash,' I said, trying to laugh it off.

There was another silence.

'Vanessa and I will be okay. We're just taking it one day at a time. Prayer, looking at the alternatives... adoption maybe. I don't know. I just always thought we would have kids straightaway. I never, ever thought that this would happen. Never. It was something that happened to other people. On television but not in real life and especially, not to me. A preacher. Somehow the biblical entreaty to be fruitful and multiply doesn't quite have the same ring now.'

He laughed at his own joke.

'Mark... '

'You've got to laugh. Jesus laughed too, believe it or not.'

The women arrived with a yawning Yanis. They put him in his favourite position on the blanket in the middle of the room. He started rolling from side to side.

'He'll be crawling soon,' Vanessa said.

'Most definitely,' Kemi said.

My son smiled, showing off his two new teeth and saliva-making abilities.

23

A month later, we exchanged contracts on our new house, although we still hadn't found a buyer for our flat. The wedding plans were coming on. I was doing better at deserving my title of dependable rock in my home. Kemi was on target for her desired weight loss for the wedding day and Yanis had started crawling. I still went past my mother's house sometimes but with no contact. And I'd met up once with Jack Morris. At work, our negotiations with the Liberian minister had stalled and *SWA* were proving increasingly difficult to please with their demands for social projects.

I was still reading my Bible and had even started attending baptismal classes at the church. It was one evening after one of those classes that I came home, got down on my knees and confessed to God that I was a sinner and that I had a lot of pride in my heart. I admitted to God that I didn't have all the answers, that I needed him. I'd said the sinner's prayer before when I was trying to please my wife. This time, it was because I really wanted to do it for myself.

I got up from my knees and went straight into the lounge ready to ask Kemi to forgive me for being so difficult during those trying early months after Yanis was born. I opened my mouth – and a babble of nonsense came out.

'Zack, you're speaking in tongues,' Kemi said, her eyes shining.

I didn't want to speak in tongues. I found it disconcerting, too noisy. But when I described to Kemi what had just happened, telling her that I'd prayed to ask God to forgive my proud heart, she told me I'd get over it.

So, all in all, life was pretty good. I was slowly coming to terms with my mother's rejection. I didn't think the hurt would ever go away but I consoled myself with the thought that I at least knew a lot more about my background. I also spent a lot of my time reading up on Eritrea. I hoped to go there one day.

Then, one mid-September morning, I was walking past a newsagent's when the headlines: *The Diamond Mines, Liberia and the Rhodenburg Bribe* screamed at me. I almost threw the change at the newsagent and ran out of the shop, my eyes scanning the newspaper pages.

The article referred to Rhodenburg's work in China and our failed enterprises in East Timor and Sarajevo. It went on to describe Rhodenburg's intent to single-handedly restructure Liberia's diamond mines with the aim of getting sole access to the diamond mines. It quoted a statement from one Zack Kariba, Rhodenburg Senior Legal Adviser, who was in the process of drawing up a binding contract that would be made with the new government. It also mentioned one Andy Hunt, a so-called strategist, who was so desperate to get Rhodenburg's hands on Liberia's diamonds that he offered bribes to an aide to Liberia's transitional Minister for Lands, Mines and Energy. Except that the minister found out and was furious. Rhodenburg, the newspaper went on, was supposed to be working with *Save West Africa*, a charity that was so concerned about Rhodenburg's intentions in Liberia that it felt it had no choice but to announce the truth to the whole world.

Grace. It was her. She did this.

I rushed into the office, fighting my way through the reporters milling outside. Richard's face was grim, as was Maxine's. Andy was nowhere to be seen.

'I told you, but you wouldn't listen,' Maxine hissed.

'Zack, Maxine – in my office. Now!' Richard announced.

'Did you imagine you were so irresistible that I would jeopardise my job and reputation for you?' Maxine smirked at me behind Richard's back.

During the brief meeting in Richard's office it became obvious I no longer had a job at Rhodenburg. The national newspaper article had ensured that by linking my name as well as Andy's to their accusations.

'I want to know everything there is to know. Start talking,' Richard ordered us.

I said a quick prayer for strength and wisdom.

'Did you or did you not know about this? One of you had better start talking. Do you realise what's happened here? You've put Rhodenburg's integrity on the line.'

'I was told that Andy had that intention... of bribing the aide,' I began, 'But it was unsubstantiated. I had no way of proving it without letting him know that he was under investigation.'

'And you didn't think to notify me about these allegations?'

'I wanted to be sure of the facts,' I replied.

Richard turned to Maxine.

'Maxine. You're awfully quiet today.'

'It's like Zack said. We wanted to be sure of the facts before coming to you.'

'And you waited and waited and waited... and while you were waiting, this happens. We do not even have a case against the newspaper because Andy, the chief suspect, has disappeared.'

Maxine tried to speak again, but Richard ignored her.

'I want the two of you out of this building in the next 30 minutes. After that, if I see you within 500 yards of this building, I'll have you both arrested.'

We cleared our desks and were escorted out of the building by security guards. Later that day, I watched the re-run of my exit on the evening news. I seethed with anger. How were we going to live? We'd just exchanged contracts on a mortgage based on two decent incomes. My name would for ever be synonymous with Rhodenburg and the Liberia affair. The thought of doing battle with the Law Society to clear my name and restore my professional credibility did not fill me with any enthusiasm. It would be a long, drawn-out and expensive process. And what would the church say?

Damn that woman! She was my thorn in the flesh.

* * *

Kemi turned off the television.

'I've had enough,' she said. The phone rang again, as it had been doing all day. We let it go to voicemail. The only people we took calls from were Femi, Michael and Vanessa. And Jack Morris. We reassured them all that we were fine.

'I'm sorry, Kemi.'

'Don't be silly. We'll lock ourselves in the house for the next few days and I'll defy anyone at work to say anything to me.'

'How are we going to manage? Our savings are not going to last for ever and the wedding... how will we manage?'

I put my head in my hands in despair. In one fell swoop, that woman had destroyed my career and livelihood.

Yanis T was trying to pull himself up at my legs. I took him in my arms and peered through the curtains. One or two reporters were still skulking around. God knows what the neighbours were thinking.

I couldn't sleep. At midnight, I crept out of bed, went downstairs and called Liberia. She picked it up on the first ring.

'Grace?'

'Zack, I'm sorry. The reporter took what I said about you out of context. I just wanted to stop Andy, that's all. I didn't know it was going to be front page news.'

'Don't lie to me, Grace. You've destroyed my career. I hope you're happy.'

'I'm sorry, Zachary. I really am. I didn't know it would turn out like this. Honest.'

I wasn't sure I could believe her, but I also saw this as the chance to do something that had been on my mind for a while.

'Listen. You had no right to kill my child. No right at all. You almost destroyed me, just like you're doing with my career now... '

'Zachary—'

'My name is Zack. Well, I hope you're happy. I wish you well,' I said and hung up. I went back to bed and wrapped my arms around my sleeping wife. But sleep did not come.

Epilogue

I'm coming to the end of my story, although two whole years have gone by since that dreadful sleepless night. Should I call my tale *The Downfall of Zack Kariba*? Or *The Making of Zack Kariba*? Maybe it'll just be *Zack's Story* and I'll let you decide how things have really turned out.

Kemi and I didn't leave our flat for a whole week after the newspaper article broke. Reporters made it impossible. Andy was never found. Since the day we were escorted out of the office building, Maxine hasn't made contact with me. It was a relief. I never told Kemi about her tactics to get me into bed with her. I figured that was best left untold.

We had a great church blessing/wedding. The church, Kemi's family and all the usual suspects contributed financially towards it, bless them all. Jack Morris was my best man. He looked so proud. Foluke flew in from Nigeria. She's engaged to a pastor, believe it or not. Altogether a more promising prospect. Vanessa and Mark do not have kids yet but they are still hoping and praying. They are so good with Yanis and sometimes take him off for the day.

I struggled to get work after being dismissed and even thought about setting up my own law firm, but somehow it didn't appeal. In the end, I thought I would play house until I figured out what to do. It took the pressure off Kemi and she's done so well in her career. They found a venue in Leeds for *World Star Baby* and it was a smash hit. As I write, she's European Director for her company, a position she's revelled in for the past year. Perhaps more surprising is what's happened with Sharronne. Kemi invited her to church – and she just kept coming! She now comes to church regularly, although at this point is refusing to make a commitment to Jesus. It drives Kemi nuts! I think you could say they're friends now, though Kemi refuses to put a label on their relationship.

I waited a long while after the Liberia affair before doing a little bit of legal stuff for people at church. It keeps me sane. I've also been writing a few articles for professional magazines, which seem to be well received. I'm happy for now, though I feel ready for another adventure. I think a lot about Liberia. The memory of what I saw in the displacement camp hasn't faded. I know the risks, but I would like to go back to see what I can do to alleviate the suffering I witnessed. But first – Eritrea. I've been reading up on it and we're all going there in a few months' time as a family. We're calling it our family journey of discovery. Of course, I think about my father sometimes, although Jack refuses to tell me any more about him. He says I should let sleeping dogs lie.

Yanis is a great little kid. Loud, demanding and full of energy, just like his mum. I'm ready for another – but Kemi's not convinced. Yet.

Gail had a health scare last year, but came through, thank God. She and Femi are a big part of our lives and I want it to be that way for a long time to come.

I'm still learning and growing in God. My faith in God has given me the kind of security I always dreamed about. I know I've still got lots to learn. Pride is always going to be a bit of an issue for me, I know that. And the other big need is for me to learn to do forgiveness. My need to blame and judge others is an ongoing shadow in my life. My goal is one day to be able to say I forgive Grace, and truly mean it.

Talking of forgiveness, I still occasionally walk past a certain house in a nice neighbourhood hoping to catch a glimpse of a certain woman or my three unknown siblings. But even that need feels less urgent than it was. Whatever happens, there'll always be a space in my life for my mother if she decides she wants it.

Other than that, I'm just taking it one day at a time. I don't know what the future holds but I'm assured that, as a child of God, it's all in his hands. A cliché, I know. But I believe it and it's fine with me.

Help with reading the Bible

SCRIPTURE UNION produces a wide range of publications, many of which help people understand the Bible.

You might like to request free samplers from our range of quarterly personal Bible-reading guides:

CLOSER TO GOD – experiential, relational, radical and dynamic, this publication takes a creative and reflective approach to Bible reading with an emphasis on renewal.

DAILY BREAD – to help you enjoy, explore and apply the Bible. Practical comments relate the Bible to everyday life, combined with information and meditation panels to give deeper understanding.

ENCOUNTER WITH GOD – provides a thought-provoking, in-depth approach to Bible reading, relating Biblical truth to contemporary issues. The writers are experienced Bible teachers, often well known.

To request a free copy or find out more:

- phone SU's mail order line: 0845 0706006
- email info@scriptureunion.org.uk
- fax 01908 856020
- log on to www.scriptureunion.org.uk
- write to SU Mail Order, PO Box 5148, Milton Keynes MLO, MK2 2YX

Taking it further

If you'd like to think further about some of the issues raised in this book – either by yourself or in the context of a small discussion group or reading group – then go to www.scriptureunion.org.uk/zack, where you'll find some helpful starter questions and discussion pointers.

Getting advice

For men and women dealing with pregnancies and abortion in the UK and other countries go to:
www.careconfidential.com or www.pregnancy.org.uk

Additionally, men dealing with crisis pregnancies and abortion in the UK can ring (free and confidentially) 0800 028 2228.

The two books given to Zack (see page 38) are:

Answers to Tough Questions about the Christian Faith, published by Authentic Lifestyle.

Mere Christianity by CS Lewis, published by HarperCollins.

Zack's Story is a sequel to Kemi's Journal

KEMI'S JOURNAL
of life, love and everything
Abidemi Sanusi

Welcome to Kemi's world – a slice of zany London life as only a twenty-something born-again believer might see it. Meet the cast: Kemi's friend-with-all-the-answers Vanessa and Vanessa's perfect fiancé Mark; Kemi's marketing company boss Amanda and colleague Robert, who conduct a whirlwind office romance; Pastor Michael and the Sanctifieds – not a boy band but her friends at church. And Zack, Kemi's boyfriend from life BC (Before Church). Jesus is very much there, too, as Kemi's friend and confidant. And the Bible, which inspires and freaks her out by turn.

In between weeping bouts in the office loo, witnessing on the streets of Camden and winning promotion for her Singing Diapers Star Baby campaign, Kemi is struggling bigtime. Could she really be pregnant...?